INTO THE UNKNOWN

BHARAT'S JOURNEY

HARDIK TIWARI

Made with ❤ on the Notion Press Platform
www.notionpress.com

For the dreamers and explorers, who seek the extraordinary in the ordinary. This story is for those who listen to the whispers of mystery and follow where they lead.

And to my family and friends, thank you for your constant support and belief in me throughout this journey.

Contents

Foreword *vii*

Prologue *ix*

1. The Phantom Ship 1
2. The Midnight Quest 8
3. Into The Unknown 16
4. Aryavrata 25
5. The Prophecy Unfolds 36
6. The First Temple 49
7. The Trials 62
8. Raktashak 71
9. The Shadow Realm 82
10. Sankalp Shila 91
11. Shadows Of The Past 100
12. The Saviour Of Realms 106

The Whisper of Shadows 119

Foreword

Into the Unknown: Bharat's Journey started as a simple idea—an ordinary man drawn into extraordinary circumstances. As I explored Bharat's story, it became something more: a tale of adventure, mystery, and self-discovery.

This novel is not just about the places Bharat visits or the challenges he faces. It's about the inner journey, the quiet moments of doubt, courage, and growth. I've always been fascinated by the boundary between the known and the unknown, and this story is my way of exploring that fine line.

The themes of this book—sacrifice, curiosity, and the pull of unseen forces—reflect the complexities of life itself. I hope Bharat's journey will resonate with readers, offering not only an escape into a world of magic and mystery but also a reflection on our own roles in the grand adventure of life.

Thank you for embarking on this journey with Bharat and me. I hope you enjoy the adventure as much as I enjoyed creating it.

— Hardik Tiwari

Prologue

The Whispering Winds

The sea had always held a mystical aura, a place where reality and myth merged. The melodic crash of waves, the beckoning horizon to nowhere and everywhere, and even the far, humming drone of the city all testified to a place where often the prosaic gave way to the magical. And on nights when the moon hung low and the smell of salt hung just a bit heavier in the air, it was as if the ocean whispered secrets—stories carried on the wind from some far-off clime and times long forgotten.

Bharat Verma, a bright and curious young journalist with an insatiable curiosity and restless spirit, had always been drawn to the mysteries of the world. He had spent many nights at the sea, lost in thoughts and contemplation of ideas about his stories. There was something in the waves that spoke to him—a place where past, present, and future meet at a point, promising glimpses of reality that were real but out of reach.

Bharat was in his late twenties, with sharp, inquisitive features that seemed to capture the light in a room just as easily as his thoughts captured ideas. His dark, unruly hair was usually left to its own devices, curling slightly at the ends as it resisted the sea breeze. He often wore a look of quiet contemplation, his deep-set brown eyes reflecting the intensity with which he viewed the world. His eyebrows, thick and expressive, moved slightly whenever he was deep in thought, almost as if they were physically drawing lines between the threads of his imagination. His nose, long and slightly arched, gave him a distinctive profile, and his lips were often pressed into a faint, thoughtful smile, as if he were on the verge of uncovering a great secret.

Bharat was of medium height, lean but not muscular, and his hands were slender, almost delicate—the hands of someone more accustomed to turning the pages of a book or scribbling notes than to manual labour. His skin was a warm, sun-kissed brown, and he wore his clothes with an air of practicality—button-up shirts with the sleeves rolled up, simple jeans, and a comfortable pair of shoes made for walking. Bharat didn't care much for appearances beyond the practicalities; his mind was always elsewhere, chasing after the next mystery or the next story that could unlock the secrets of the world.

Since childhood, Bharat had been different. While other children played carefree, Bharat's head was filled with questions that no one could easily answer. While other kids built sandcastles, he would sit on the beach and wonder what lay beneath the sand—buried treasure, lost civilizations, or the bones of creatures long extinct. He was always asking why and how, questions that adults brushed aside as fanciful, but Bharat never stopped asking them.

His parents, both pragmatists, had been both concerned and fascinated by his unusual nature. His mother often called him her "little philosopher," while his father, an engineer, worried that Bharat's head was too high in the clouds and not grounded enough in the real world. But that was just who Bharat was. His fascination with the unknown wasn't a phase—it was the essence of who he was.

From an early age, Bharat found comfort in books, especially the ones that spoke of things that couldn't be easily explained—lost cities, ancient myths, and civilizations that disappeared without a trace. As a child, he'd be the one sneaking out of bed at night, flashlight in hand, to read about the Bermuda Triangle, Atlantis, or the Voynich manuscript. These stories weren't just entertainment for Bharat; they were fuel for his curiosity, igniting a fire inside him that burned with a desire to know what lay beyond the veil of the ordinary.

This yearning followed him into adulthood. Journalism, for Bharat, was a natural fit. It was a profession where curiosity was not just encouraged but necessary. He had a gift for unearthing the stories no one else wanted to cover—the strange, the bizarre, the unexplainable. In his years as a journalist, he had earned a reputation for diving into the odd and mysterious. He loved the stories that everyone else dismissed: a haunting in a forgotten village, an unexplained light in the sky over a remote town, or an ancient curse that still held sway over the ruins of a fort.

But despite the thrill of the chase, Bharat always felt like something was missing. No matter how many stories he uncovered, there was always a nagging feeling that there was something more—something just out of reach, waiting for him to discover it. It wasn't about fame or recognition; it was about a deeper truth, something that could explain the world in a way that no one else could.

And so, Bharat found himself at the edge of the sea more often than not. The sea had always called to him, its vastness a mirror of the unexplored depths of his own mind. It was where he came to think, to puzzle out the mysteries that eluded him. The rhythmic crash of the waves was like a mantra, soothing and stirring at the same time. On some nights, he would sit on the sand for hours, staring out at the water, his mind lost in thought.

Nights by the sea felt different to him than any other time. It was as if the darkness stripped away the distractions of the world, leaving only the raw power of the ocean and the stars above. The moon would cast a pale glow on the water, turning the waves into silver ribbons that stretched out into the horizon. The wind would tug at his clothes, teasing strands of his hair, as if urging him to move, to act, to follow its call.

Sometimes, he would feel a strange presence, as if he wasn't alone on the shore. He would turn, expecting to see someone standing beside him, but there was never anyone there. The shadows, though, seemed alive. They shifted and swayed with a rhythm of their own, as if the night itself was watching him, waiting for something. Bharat was no stranger to such feelings—he had felt them many times in his life, but here, by the sea, they were stronger than ever. It was as if the very air was charged with a kind of magic that couldn't be explained, only felt.

The sea was both his muse and his mystery. It was constant, yet ever-changing. There were nights when the water was calm, lapping gently at the shore, and other nights when it was wild and fierce, the waves crashing with such force that Bharat could feel the ground tremble beneath him. But whether the sea was peaceful or angry, Bharat always felt that it held secrets—secrets that it was waiting to reveal to him.

For weeks, there had been a growing tension in the air, something that Bharat couldn't quite explain. It started as a subtle feeling, like an itch at the back of his mind, but it grew stronger with each passing day. He would be walking along the shore, the cool water lapping at his feet, and suddenly, everything would go still—the wind, the waves, the distant sounds of the city. It was as if the world was holding its breath, waiting for something to happen.

And then there were the dreams.

They had started a few weeks ago, vivid and strange. In these dreams, Bharat found himself in places he had never been before—places that didn't exist, at least not in the world he knew. He dreamed of sailing across stormy seas, the wind whipping at his face as waves rose like mountains around him. He dreamed of walking through ancient forests, the trees so tall that they seemed to touch the sky. And always, there was the sense of something watching him, something just out of sight, waiting for him to find it.

In the dreams, he felt a strange mixture of fear and excitement, as though he was on the verge of discovering something monumental. But when he woke up, the feeling would linger, gnawing at him throughout the day, pulling his thoughts back to the dreams no matter how hard he tried to focus on his work. His editor, Mr. Rao, had noticed the change in him and suggested he take some time off. Bharat had tried to explain what he was feeling, but how could he put it into words? How could he explain that he felt as though the universe was aligning, preparing him for something he couldn't yet understand?

The dreams, the feelings, the sense of anticipation—it all came to a head one evening. Bharat had been standing at the edge of the water, his feet sinking into the cool sand, when he felt it again—that pull. It was stronger than ever, like a hand reaching out to him from across the waves, beckoning him to follow.

The wind picked up, tugging at his clothes, and the air seemed to thrum with energy. He could feel his heart pounding in his chest, each beat matching the rhythm of the waves as they crashed against the shore. The sky above had turned from indigo to a deep, velvety black, the stars flickering like beacons in the distance. The moon hung low in the sky, casting a pale glow over the water, and the sea, once calm, seemed to shift and change before his eyes.

It was at that moment that Bharat knew—something was coming. He didn't know what it was, or how it would change his life, but he could feel it in his bones. It was as if the world itself was holding its breath, waiting for him to take the next step.

He closed his eyes and took a deep breath, letting the cool night air fill his lungs. The wind whispered to him, soft and insistent, carrying with it the weight of too many stories untold. It urged him to listen, to look at the signs that had been laid before him.

When he opened his eyes again, he knew without a doubt that his life was about to change.

The winds off the sea were calling, and for the very first time, so was Bharat.

CHAPTER I

The Phantom Ship

The city of Mumbai awoke under the veil of early morning mist. The streets, usually thrumming with the pulse of millions, were momentarily calm, the air thick with humidity and the promise of another scorching day. A gentle haze clung to the horizon where the sea met the city, blurring the distinction between the waking world and the slumbering ocean. The air was heavy, almost syrupy, as it hung low, carrying the smell of salt, diesel, and a faint trace of something metallic—an invisible undercurrent of the bustling city.

Bharat Verma was no exception to the city's routine. Dressed in light, comfortable clothes—an old blue shirt and jeans—he had slipped into the habit of early morning walks by the sea, a ritual that centered his thoughts before the city consumed him with its chaotic rhythms. His footsteps echoed softly against the concrete path along Marine Drive, blending seamlessly with the symphony of the waves crashing against the rocks. The rhythmic sound, constant yet ever-changing, soothed his mind, preparing him for the day ahead.

Today, however, Bharat felt a subtle tension in the air, something unspoken that gnawed at his consciousness. It wasn't just the humidity that clung to his skin—it was something more profound, something stirring beneath the surface. Normally, Bharat's walks ended with him returning to his small, cluttered apartment to brew his first cup of coffee and settle into the day's work. But today, his feet took him in a different direction, toward a familiar café just steps away from the shore.

The café was small, nestled discreetly at the end of a narrow street. Its exterior was modest, with a weathered wooden sign that had faded over the years, though the painted words "Sea Breeze Café" could still be read. Inside, the place was a cosy haven, a blend of the smell of fresh coffee and the musty scent of old books that lined the back shelves. Dim yellow lights cast a soft glow over the dark wooden furniture, and the hum of conversation mingled with the clattering of cups and the hissing of the espresso machine.

Bharat had first discovered the café years ago and had quickly made it his sanctuary. It was the kind of place where time seemed to slow down, where the noise of the city outside was muffled into a distant hum. Here, amidst the quiet clatter of dishes and the occasional low murmur of conversation, Bharat could escape into his thoughts, free from the pressures of his daily routine.

"Good morning, Bharat," a familiar voice greeted him as he stepped inside.

It was Meena, the middle-aged barista who had worked at the café for as long as Bharat could remember. Her salt-and-pepper hair was tied back in a loose bun, and her warm smile was as welcoming as the scent of freshly brewed coffee that filled the air.

"Morning, Meena," Bharat replied, his own smile pulling at the corners of his mouth. "The usual, please."

Meena nodded, already turning toward the espresso machine. "One strong black coffee coming right up."

Bharat made his way to his favourite seat in the corner by the large window, where he had the perfect view of the street outside. The early morning light filtered through the mist, casting soft shadows on the pavement. There was something about this hour, Bharat thought, that made the café feel almost magical. It was a quiet interlude before the city awoke fully—a moment of peace before the world outside rushed back in.

He placed his worn leather bag on the floor beside his seat and retrieved his laptop, setting it on the table. As he waited for his coffee, he opened the laptop and began scanning the day's headlines. It was a routine he had developed over the years—catching up on the latest news before diving into his own work. Most of the stories were the usual fare: political scandals, economic forecasts, celebrity gossip. Bharat's eyes moved across the screen with practised detachment, his mind already wandering to the next story he hoped to write.

But then, something caught his eye—a headline that made him pause, his heart skipping a beat.

MYSTERY SHIP APPEARS ON JUHU BEACH OVERNIGHT: AUTHORITIES BAFFLED.

The words seemed to pulse on the screen. Bharat blinked, feeling a rush of anticipation as he clicked on the article. The page loaded slowly, teasing him with the promise of a tale unlike any other. When the article finally appeared, he read it in growing excitement.

"A huge, ancient ship has mysteriously washed up onto the shores of Juhu Beach, its weatherworn hull rising ominously out of the sand. The vessel, appearing seemingly overnight, looks like a relic from a time long forgotten. Authorities are at a loss to explain its sudden appearance, and experts are baffled by how such a large ship could arrive without being detected."

Bharat's heart raced as he scrolled through the article. The ship had been discovered at dawn, its massive silhouette casting long, jagged shadows across the sand.

Fishermen had been the first to spot it as they set out early in the morning, their boats veering away from the looming structure that had appeared as if from nowhere.

The description of the ship sent a chill down Bharat's spine. The vessel was enormous, with tattered sails that hung limply, as if torn apart by the ravages of time. The wood of the hull was dark and weathered, covered in barnacles and seaweed—evidence that the ship had spent decades, if not centuries, lost at sea. And yet, it bore no markings, no flag, no name. It was as though the ship had come from a place that no longer existed—a ghost from another era, set adrift in the present.

The article continued, quoting historians and marine experts, none of whom had an explanation. Some speculated that the ship had been carried to shore by a freak storm or a rare oceanic current. Others suggested it was a hoax, though the size and condition of the ship made that seem unlikely. Theories ranged from the plausible to the absurd, but one thing was clear: the ship was a mystery, and it had captured the imagination of the entire city.

Bharat leaned back in his chair, his mind racing. Almost, he could picture the ship towering above the beach, a relic from a forgotten past. This was exactly the kind of story he had been waiting for—something more than just another assignment, something that tugged at the edges of his curiosity and called him to action.

His thoughts were interrupted by the arrival of his coffee. Meena placed the steaming cup on the table, her expression curious. "You seem deep in thought today, Bharat. Anything exciting happening?"

Bharat glanced up, offering her a smile as he gestured to the screen. "You could say that. A ship has appeared out of nowhere on Juhu Beach—an old, weathered vessel, like something straight out of a storybook. Authorities are baffled."

Meena raised an eyebrow, her hands resting on her hips. "A ghost ship? Now that's something you don't hear about every day."

Bharat chuckled, though there was an edge of excitement in his voice. "Exactly. It's a mystery, and I can't shake the feeling that there's something more to it."

Meena nodded, her expression thoughtful. "Well, if anyone can get to the bottom of it, it's you. Just be careful, alright? Mysteries like that... they have a way of pulling people in deeper than they expect."

Bharat smiled, but her words lingered in his mind. As Meena returned to the counter, he took a deep breath, his fingers tapping lightly against the side of his coffee cup. There was something about this story—something that felt different from the others. It was more than just a curiosity; it was a calling. And Bharat knew that he had to follow it, wherever it led.

Without a second thought, he finished his coffee in one swift gulp, the bitter liquid jolting him into action. He snapped his laptop shut and gathered his belongings, his mind already racing ahead to the beach, to the ship that awaited him. The sea had always called to him, whispering its secrets through the waves. But now, that call had grown louder, more insistent, urging him forward.

As he stepped out of the café and into the street, Bharat could feel the rising excitement in his chest. The sun had climbed higher in the sky, burning away the last remnants of the morning mist, but Bharat hardly noticed. His thoughts were consumed with the image of the ship, looming over the beach like a watchful sentinel. There was a pull to it, something that tugged at the very core of his being.

He hailed an auto-rickshaw and climbed in, giving the driver quick instructions to take him to Juhu Beach. The city had begun to awaken in earnest now, the streets filling with the familiar sounds of honking cars, shouting vendors, and the general hum of life. As the rickshaw weaved through the morning traffic, Bharat's mind wandered back to the article. He couldn't shake the feeling that this was more than just a simple mystery. It felt almost like a sign, as though the ship had appeared for a reason—as though it had been waiting for him.

The ride to the beach was slow, the rickshaw rattling as it swerved between cars and buses. Bharat tapped his fingers impatiently against his knee, eager to reach the shore and see the ship with his own eyes. The anticipation built inside him, like a pressure waiting to be released.

When they finally arrived at Juhu Beach, the sight that greeted Bharat took his breath away. A large crowd had gathered around the massive silhouette of the ship, which loomed ominously on the shore. The sun, now fully risen, cast harsh light on the sand and the sea, but the ship seemed to defy the brightness of the day. Its dark, weathered hull stood in stark contrast to the vibrant scene around it, as though it belonged to another time and place.

Police had cordoned off the area around the ship, but that hadn't stopped the crowd from gathering. People stood in clusters, murmuring in excitement and awe, their eyes fixed on the vessel that had seemingly appeared out of nowhere. Journalists with cameras slung over their shoulders hovered at the edges of the crowd, capturing every detail.

Bharat pushed his way through the throng of onlookers, his heart pounding in his chest. Up close, the ship was even more imposing than he had imagined. The hull, dark and cracked with age, rose like a monolith from the sand, its weathered wood creaking in the gentle breeze. The tattered sails, once proud, now hung in shreds, swaying slightly as if they, too, were part of the mystery.

As Bharat stared up at the ship, a strange feeling washed over him—an almost inexplicable connection, as though the ship had been waiting for him all along. It was a relic from another time, a ghost from the past, and yet it felt familiar, as though he had seen it before in some forgotten dream.

"This... is incredible," a voice next to him whispered, breaking Bharat from his reverie.

Bharat turned to see a fellow journalist, a young man with a camera hanging around his neck. His wide eyes mirrored Bharat's own awe. "You think it's real?" the young man asked, his voice barely audible over the murmur of the crowd.

Bharat nodded slowly, his gaze never leaving the ship. "It's real," he said softly. "And I'm going to find out why it's here."

The sea had always beckoned to Bharat, whispering its secrets through the waves. But now, it had delivered something tangible, something that promised answers to questions he hadn't even thought to ask. The ship was more than just a story—it was a mystery that called to him, one that would lead him into the unknown.

With a determined stride, Bharat made his way toward the police barricade, his mind already racing with possibilities. He didn't know where this story would lead him, but he was ready to follow it—ready to step into the unknown.

CHAPTER II

The Midnight Quest

The sun hung high in the sky, casting its relentless heat upon Mumbai as the city buzzed with news of the mysterious ship that had appeared overnight on the shores. The usually leisurely and vibrant Juhu Beach had been transformed into a hive of activity. Journalists, scientists, researchers, and government officials had descended upon the site, each intent on unravelling the enigma that had captured the imagination of millions.

For the citizens of Mumbai, the beach had always been a place of relaxation—where families picnicked, children played in the waves, and couples strolled hand in hand. Today, however, the atmosphere had changed. An undercurrent of tension hung in the air, as though the very fabric of reality had been disturbed. The normalcy of everyday life had been shattered by the presence of this ancient, hulking relic that now dominated the shoreline.

Bharat stood at the edge of the cordoned-off area, his brow furrowed in concentration as he watched the scene unfold before him. The ship, massive and imposing, loomed over the beach like a monument from another time. Its dark, weathered hull was like something out of an ancient legend—something that didn't belong in the here and now. Bharat couldn't help but feel the weight of history pressing down on him as he observed the ship, as though it had carried with it the echoes of the past.

He wiped the sweat from his brow and adjusted the bag slung over his shoulder, trying to ignore the heat that pressed in from all sides. Even as the sun beat down mercilessly, Bharat's focus remained locked on the ship. It wasn't just the spectacle of the ship that held his attention—it was the mystery. There was something about the ship, something beyond its physical presence, that called to him in a way he couldn't fully explain.

The air around the vessel felt charged, thick with anticipation, as though the ship itself held secrets that it was reluctant to reveal. Bharat wasn't alone in his curiosity. Dozens of scientists and researchers bustled about the site, their faces drawn in tight lines of concentration as they set up equipment and collected samples. Government officials, dressed in crisp suits and sunglasses, huddled together in groups, speaking in hushed tones as they discussed how to manage the growing public interest.

Every inch of the ship was being meticulously documented, photographed, and analysed. Teams of archaeologists and marine experts swarmed the vessel like ants, poking and prodding at its ancient timbers. The ship's hull was riddled with barnacles and other sea life, suggesting it had spent years, possibly centuries, lost at sea. And yet, here it was—washed ashore in the heart of Mumbai, as if summoned by some unseen force.

Bharat's eyes followed the researchers as they moved around the vessel, their movements methodical and precise. Every detail, every scrap of evidence, was being collected in the hopes of unravelling the mystery. The government, clearly aware of the ship's potential significance, had imposed strict restrictions on access. Only authorised personnel were allowed near the ship, and armed guards patrolled the perimeter, their presence a silent warning to anyone who might consider stepping out of line.

For Bharat, this was both frustrating and intriguing. As a journalist, he was accustomed to being at the forefront of major stories, digging deep into the facts and uncovering the truth. But here, he found himself on the outside, watching as others conducted the investigation. He knew that the answers he sought were locked away within the ship, but getting close enough to find them would be no easy task.

He sighed and ran a hand through his hair, which was damp with sweat from the midday heat. His mind raced with questions, each one more pressing than the last. How had the ship arrived here? Where did it come from? And most importantly, what secrets did it hold?

Determined not to waste any time, Bharat decided to make the most of the situation. If he couldn't get on the ship just yet, he could at least gather information from those who had been granted access. Armed with his notepad and recorder, he scanned the crowd, looking for anyone who might be willing to talk. His eyes fell on a group of scientists who were huddled together near the ship, examining a piece of wood that had been taken from the hull.

With purposeful strides, Bharat approached the group, his notepad at the ready. He introduced himself as a journalist and politely asked if they could spare a few moments for an interview.

One of the scientists, a middle-aged man with a serious expression and a thick moustache, looked up from the sample and extended a hand. "I'm Dr. Shastri," he said, his voice deep and measured. "We're still in the early stages of our investigation, but I can share a few preliminary findings."

Bharat shook his hand and nodded, eager to hear more. "Thank you, Dr. Shastri. What have you discovered so far?"

Dr. Shastri gestured toward the sample of wood in his hand, his brow furrowing as he spoke. "This ship appears to be made of a type of timber that hasn't been used in shipbuilding for centuries. Based on our preliminary analysis, the wood dates back several hundred years—possibly more. Yet, despite its age, the wood is remarkably well-preserved. It's as though the ship has been frozen in time."

Bharat leaned in, his curiosity piqued. He scribbled notes furiously in his notepad, his mind racing with possibilities. "Frozen in time?" Bharat echoed, his voice filled with intrigue.

"Yes," Dr. Shastri continued, "It's unusual, to say the least. Ships of this age would normally have deteriorated significantly, especially if they had been exposed to the elements for any length of time. But this vessel... it's almost as if it's been protected by something—some force that has kept it intact."

Bharat was about to ask another question when a second scientist, a younger woman with short-cropped hair and sharp, analytical eyes, stepped forward. Her voice was calm, but there was a hint of excitement beneath the surface. "We've also detected traces of salt and marine organisms on the hull that are typically found in the deepest parts of the ocean—places where modern ships rarely venture."

"The deepest parts of the ocean?" Bharat asked, his pen moving rapidly across the page.

The younger scientist nodded, adjusting her glasses as she spoke. "Exactly. This suggests that the ship has spent a considerable amount of time in the open sea, far from any coastline. It's likely been drifting for years, perhaps even centuries. And yet, there are no records of any ship like this being in the area. No one saw it approaching the shore."

Bharat's mind raced as he tried to reconcile the information. "How could a ship like this, with such an ancient design, suddenly appear on a modern beach without anyone noticing its approach?"

Dr. Shastri shook his head, a look of bewilderment on his face. "That's the million-dollar question, isn't it? There are no records of any ship matching this description in the area, and no one reported seeing it until it was already on the beach. It's as if it materialised out of thin air."

The younger scientist chimed in, her voice laced with skepticism. "We've considered the possibility that it might be a replica or an elaborate hoax, but the level of detail, the age of the materials... everything points to this being an authentic, historical vessel. If it is a hoax, it's the most convincing one I've ever seen."

Bharat nodded thoughtfully, his pen still moving across the page. The more he learned, the more questions he had. The ship's sudden appearance, its ancient design, the mystery surrounding its origins—it was all too much to ignore. This wasn't just another story. This was something far bigger, something that could change everything.

As he thanked the scientists for their time, Bharat couldn't shake the feeling that the answers he sought were just within reach—if only he could get closer to the ship.

The crowd of onlookers had continued to grow throughout the day, drawn by the spectacle of the ancient vessel. Families, tourists, and locals gathered at the edge of the cordoned-off area, their faces alight with curiosity and wonder. The murmur of voices filled the air, punctuated by the occasional shout from a child or the click of a camera.

The ship had become a magnet for attention, a mystery that seemed to grow with each passing hour.

And yet, despite the excitement, there was an undercurrent of tension. The government, keen to maintain control of the situation, had increased security around the site. More guards had been deployed, their expressions stern as they patrolled the perimeter. Barriers had been erected to keep the public at a safe distance, and the beach, once a place of freedom and openness, had become a restricted zone, guarded by the state.

For Bharat, this only fueled his determination. He could feel the story pulling him in, drawing him closer with every passing moment. The ship was the key, he knew it. But getting on board was another matter entirely. With security tighter than ever, any attempt to approach the vessel during the day would be met with immediate resistance. He needed a plan—one that would allow him to slip past the guards and explore the ship without interference.

As Bharat stood at the edge of the crowd, watching the guards pace back and forth along the perimeter, an idea began to form in his mind. The security was tight during the day, with hundreds of people milling about, but at night, when the beach was empty, the situation might be different. The darkness would provide cover, and with fewer guards on duty, the chances of slipping through undetected would be much higher.

Bharat knew it was a risky plan. If he were caught, he could face serious consequences, not only from the authorities but also from his employer. But the allure of the mystery was too strong to resist. The ship called to him, its secrets tantalisingly close yet frustratingly out of reach. He had to know what lay within its ancient walls, even if it meant bending a few rules to get there.

That evening, as the sun dipped below the horizon and the shadows lengthened across the sand, Bharat prepared himself for the task ahead. He gathered a flashlight, a small backpack with essentials, and his trusty notepad. He dressed in dark clothing to blend in with the night and waited patiently for the beach to empty.

The atmosphere had shifted. The once-crowded beach was now eerily silent, save for the rhythmic crash of the waves against the shore. The air had grown cooler, the oppressive heat of the day replaced by a crisp breeze that carried the scent of salt and sand. The moon hung low in the sky, casting its pale light across the water, illuminating the ship's massive silhouette.

Bharat watched from a distance as the guards continued their patrols. They moved slowly, their flashlights cutting through the darkness as they scanned the perimeter. But there were gaps in their movements—moments when their attention was focused elsewhere, when they turned away from the ship. These were the moments Bharat had been waiting for.

With his heart pounding in his chest, Bharat began his approach. He moved carefully, sticking to the shadows, his footsteps muffled by the soft sand. The sound of the waves crashing against the shore provided a natural cover, masking any noise he might make. As he drew closer to the ship, he could feel the tension in the air, a sense of foreboding that sent shivers down his spine.

Finally, he reached the edge of the cordoned-off area. The ship loomed before him, its dark silhouette standing out against the starry sky. Up close, the vessel was even more imposing, its massive hull rising like a fortress from the sand. Bharat took a deep breath, steeling himself for what was to come.

The guards were nearby, but their attention was elsewhere, giving him the window of opportunity he needed. With a silent prayer, Bharat slipped under the barrier and made his way toward the ship. The ground beneath his feet was firm, the sand giving way to the solid wood of the ship's ramp. He placed a hand on the ancient timbers, feeling the rough texture of the wood beneath his fingers. The ship felt alive, as though it were a living entity, waiting for him to uncover its secrets.

Bharat knew that this was only the beginning. The real challenge lay ahead, within the dark, labyrinthine corridors of the ship. But he was ready. He had come too far to turn back now. As he climbed aboard, his flashlight illuminating the path ahead, Bharat felt a surge of excitement mixed with a touch of fear. The unknown awaited him, and he was about to step into its depths.

CHAPTER III

Into the Unknown

The moon hung high in the sky, casting its silvery light across the desolate beach. Bharat's footsteps echoed softly on the wooden planks as he made his way up the ramp and onto the deck of the mysterious ship. The night air was cool but heavy with the scent of salt and decay, a potent reminder of the vessel's long, forgotten journey through time and the elements. His breath fogged the air as he exhaled slowly, the cold biting at his skin. The ship loomed before him like a shadow of the past, an eerie and silent witness to centuries of untold stories.

The moonlight cast long, sharp shadows across the deck, illuminating the ship in a ghostly glow that sent shivers down Bharat's spine. The light shimmered off the weathered timbers, giving the whole scene an otherworldly quality, as if the ship was more than just a relic—something alive, pulsing with forgotten memories.

As he stood there, the full weight of what he was doing settled over him. He was alone on an ancient, possibly cursed, ship that had appeared out of nowhere, with no one around to offer any explanation or assistance. It was the kind of situation that would have made a less determined person turn back, but Bharat's curiosity was too strong. He had come this far, and he wasn't about to let fear hold him back.

The night was quiet, save for the rhythmic lapping of the waves against the hull and the distant, faint cries of nocturnal seabirds. Bharat could hear his own heartbeat in his ears, quick and steady, matching the pulse of the ocean.

He adjusted the strap of his small backpack, feeling the weight of the flashlight inside, his notepad, and the faint hope that he might find some answers aboard this strange vessel.

Bharat's mind raced as he flicked on his flashlight and swept the beam across the deck. The ship was enormous, its deck stretching out before him like a vast, empty plain, devoid of any sign of life. The wood beneath his feet was weathered and cracked, covered in patches of moss and barnacles that seemed to glisten eerily in the dim light. The air was damp, and each breath tasted of salt and brine, filling his lungs with the sensation of a world long lost at sea.

His eyes followed the path of the light, taking in the ruined majesty of the ship's masts towering above him, their tattered sails fluttering in the cold night breeze. They hung like the broken wings of a giant, decrepit bird, once majestic but now grounded and helpless.

The ship creaked beneath him, the wood groaning under the weight of centuries, and Bharat couldn't help but feel a sense of unease creeping into his bones.

"What have you gotten yourself into, Bharat?" he muttered to himself, his voice barely a whisper in the oppressive silence. The words fell flat, swallowed by the vastness of the ship and the unrelenting solitude of the night. There were no answers here—only more questions.

He moved forward cautiously, his flashlight revealing more of the ship's features. The deck was cluttered with all manner of debris—rusted chains, broken barrels, and the decayed remains of what might have once been crates or chests. Everything was coated in a fine layer of grime and salt, as though it had been untouched for centuries. Bharat crouched down, brushing his fingers against the rough, splintered wood of the deck. It felt real, solid, yet there was something about it that seemed almost unreal, as if the ship existed on the very edge of reality itself.

He stood up, casting his gaze toward the ship's helm. The ship's wheel, once the heart of the vessel, was now little more than a rotting skeleton of wood and metal. It stood like a sentinel, watching over the ship with a silent, mournful gaze. Bharat approached it slowly, his breath catching in his throat as he reached out to touch it. His fingers brushed the cold wood, and a shiver ran down his spine, as if the ship itself were warning him to turn back.

"What happened to you?" Bharat whispered, his voice barely audible over the sound of the waves. "What brought you here?"

There was no answer, only the steady rhythm of the sea. The ship was silent, its secrets locked away in the darkness, waiting for someone to uncover them. The emptiness of the ship weighed heavily on Bharat, the absence of life making the entire scene feel surreal, like a dream he couldn't wake from.

He turned away from the helm, glancing once more at the decaying masts and the tangled rigging above him. The ship had once sailed the seas with purpose and power, but now it was a hollow shell, abandoned by time. Bharat knew he needed to go deeper, to explore the bowels of the ship where the real mysteries lay hidden. His heart pounded in his chest as he made his way to the entrance of the main cabin, the door hanging loosely on its rusted hinges, creaking softly as it swayed in the breeze.

The darkness beyond was thick and impenetrable, like a void that swallowed all light. Bharat hesitated for a moment, standing on the threshold of the unknown, his mind filled with a mix of curiosity and fear. There was no telling what lay inside the ship's interior, no guarantee that he would find anything other than more questions.

But Bharat wasn't one to back down. He had spent his life chasing the unknown, driven by a thirst for answers that had led him to places most people would never dare to go. This ship was no different—just another step into the darkness, another mystery to unravel.

"Come on, Bharat. You didn't come this far just to stand here," he muttered to himself, his voice firmer this time. He took a deep breath and pushed the door open, the sound of the creaking hinges echoing through the stillness of the night.

The air inside the cabin was musty and thick, a mixture of damp wood, mildew, and something metallic and faintly sweet—like the smell of old blood. The corridor that stretched out before him was narrow, the ceiling low enough that Bharat had to duck slightly as he walked. The walls were lined with rotting wood, the boards warped and blackened with age, and cobwebs hung from the corners like tattered curtains.

Bharat's flashlight cut through the darkness, casting long shadows on the walls as he moved deeper into the ship. His footsteps were muffled on the wooden floorboards, but every creak and groan of the ship made his heart race faster. It felt as though the ship was alive, watching him, waiting for him to uncover its secrets.

The beam of his flashlight revealed a series of small, cramped rooms lining the corridor. Most of the doors were ajar, revealing glimpses of the ship's interior—rooms filled with decaying furniture, rusted tools, and other remnants of a life long forgotten. Bharat peeked inside each room as he passed, his curiosity piqued by the strange and unsettling artifacts scattered about.

In one room, he spotted a rusted lantern hanging from the ceiling, its glass cracked and covered in dust. In another, a set of old navigational tools lay on a desk, their brass surfaces tarnished and green with corrosion. A map, yellowed with age and barely legible, was pinned to the wall, its edges frayed and curled. Bharat couldn't help but wonder about the crew that had once manned this ship—who they had been, where they had come from, and what had led them to abandon their vessel.

The ship felt like a tomb, a mausoleum dedicated to a forgotten past. Bharat shivered as he walked, the oppressive silence pressing in around him like a weight on his chest.

"Who were you?" he whispered, his voice barely louder than a breath. "What happened to you?"

There was no answer, only the steady groan of the ship as it shifted with the wind. The shadows danced on the walls, twisting and writhing in the flickering light of his flashlight.

Finally, after what felt like an eternity of walking through the ship's narrow corridors, Bharat reached the end of the hallway. A large, ornately carved door loomed before him, its dark wood etched with intricate patterns that seemed to move and shift in the dim light. The door was slightly ajar, and a faint, bluish glow seeped through the crack, casting eerie shadows on the floor.

Bharat's heart pounded in his chest as he reached out to push the door open. His hand hovered over the wood for a moment, hesitating. He could feel the weight of the ship's history pressing down on him, the weight of the unknown pulling him deeper into its depths.

With a deep breath, Bharat pushed the door open and stepped inside, the sound of the creaking hinges echoing through the stillness of the room.

The room beyond was vast and filled with strange, unsettling objects. The walls were lined with shelves that sagged under the weight of dusty tomes and ancient artifacts. The air was thick with the scent of old paper, mixed with something sharper, metallic, and faintly sweet. But it was the object in the centre of the room that drew Bharat's attention—the source of the strange, bluish glow that had seeped through the door.

An ancient mirror stood in the centre of the room, its surface shimmering with a faint, ethereal light. The frame was intricately carved from silver, adorned with symbols and runes that Bharat couldn't decipher. The light from the mirror bathed the room in an otherworldly glow, casting strange, twisting shadows on the walls.

Bharat stared at the mirror, captivated by the strange light that seemed to pulse from within it. There was something about the mirror that felt both familiar and alien, as though it belonged to a different world, a different reality.

As he stepped closer, his breath caught in his throat. His fingers brushed against the smooth, cold surface of the mirror, and the light within flared, blinding him with its intensity.

Bharat stumbled back, shielding his eyes with his arm, but it was too late. The room began to spin, the walls and floor twisting and warping as if they were being pulled into the mirror's depths.

"What's happening?" Bharat gasped, panic rising in his chest as the world around him dissolved into a swirling vortex of light and shadow. He tried to pull away, to turn and run, but his body refused to obey. The mirror's pull was too strong, and before he could comprehend what was happening, he felt himself being drawn into its depths.

Everything went black.

For a moment, there was nothing—no light, no sound, no sensation. Bharat felt as though he were floating in an endless void, disconnected from the world, from time, from reality itself. Then, slowly, a new sensation began to creep over him—a warmth, a gentle breeze, the sound of rustling leaves.

Bharat opened his eyes.

He was no longer on the ship. The narrow corridors and rotting wood had been replaced by a vibrant, lush landscape. He stood in the middle of a dense forest, the trees towering above him, their leaves shimmering in the dappled sunlight. The air was fresh and cool, filled with the scent of earth and flowers, and the distant sound of birdsong echoed through the trees.

Bharat stared in disbelief at the scene before him, his mind struggling to comprehend what had just happened. The ship, the mirror, the strange light—it all felt like a dream, a surreal vision conjured by his imagination. But the ground beneath his feet, the cool breeze on his skin, the rustling of the leaves—these were real, tangible, impossible to deny.

He stood in the middle of a vast, ancient forest. The trees around him were like giants, their trunks thick and twisted with age. Their bark was dark, almost black, and their leaves shimmered with a strange iridescence that caught the light of the sun in unexpected ways. Some of the trees were covered in thick vines that coiled around their trunks like serpents, while others were adorned with flowers that glowed faintly in the shade.

The forest floor was a mosaic of colours—soft mosses of emerald green, patches of flowers in hues of purple and gold, and the dark, rich soil that seemed to pulse with life. The air was filled with the scent of earth, leaves, and something else, something sweet and exotic that Bharat couldn't quite place.

Above him, the canopy of leaves filtered the sunlight, creating patterns of light and shadow that danced across the forest floor. The sound of rustling leaves and distant birdsong filled the air, giving the place an almost serene quality. Yet, there was something unsettling about the silence that lay beneath it all, as if the forest itself was watching, waiting for something to happen.

Bharat took a step forward, his foot sinking slightly into the soft earth. Every movement felt tentative, like stepping into a dream that could vanish at any moment. He glanced around, trying to get his bearings, but the forest stretched out in every direction, endless and unfamiliar.

"Where am I?" Bharat whispered, his voice barely audible over the sounds of the forest. He turned in a slow circle, taking in the unfamiliar landscape, the vibrant colours, the towering trees. This was not Mumbai, not the world he knew. This was somewhere else, somewhere beyond the boundaries of the reality he had always known.

The realisation hit him like a punch to the gut, leaving him breathless and disoriented. He had crossed over into another world, a place that defied all logic and reason. And now, as he stood in the heart of this strange, beautiful forest, Bharat knew that his journey was only just beginning.

With no other option, he began to walk, his footsteps crunching softly on the forest floor. Every step took him deeper into the unknown, and with each passing moment, the mysteries of this new world seemed to multiply. The ship had been the beginning, the portal that had opened the door to a reality beyond his understanding.

The trees towered above him, their branches weaving together to create a canopy that blocked out most of the sky. The light that filtered through was soft and golden, casting everything in an ethereal glow. The air was thick with the scent of flowers and earth, and as Bharat walked, he couldn't shake the feeling that he was being watched.

And Bharat was determined to uncover its secrets, no matter where the path might lead.

CHAPTER IV

Aryavrata

The ship stood silent on the shore, a relic of another time, its dark silhouette stark against the moonlit sky. The winds had died down, leaving the beach in an unnatural stillness. All was quiet, except for a faint, almost imperceptible whisper that seemed to emanate from the ship itself.

Within the shadows that clung to the ancient timbers, something stirred. A figure, barely more than a wisp of darkness, moved silently across the deck, its presence hidden from the eyes of those who had been drawn to the mystery of the ship. The figure paused near the ship's helm, where the remnants of the wheel stood like a monument to forgotten journeys.

It gazed out toward the horizon, its form flickering like a flame in the wind. The voice that emerged from the shadows was low and guttural, barely more than a breath. "So, he has found his way to Aryavrata," it muttered, the words laced with a mixture of anticipation and malice. "The time has come... the Sankalp Shila is within reach."

The shadow shifted, its form elongating and contracting, as if contemplating the path ahead. "He does not yet know what awaits him. But soon, he will. And when he does... I will be ready."

With that, the shadow dissipated into the night, leaving the ship as still and silent as before, its secrets hidden beneath the weight of centuries.

Bharat wandered deeper into the heart of Aryavrata, each step echoing in the quiet stillness of this new world. The trees, massive and ancient, seemed to hum with life.

Their trunks were broad, almost unyielding, with gnarled roots that tangled through the ground like an endless network. The foliage above him formed a thick canopy, the leaves glowing faintly with a soft, ethereal light. The sensation of the air here was different too—it was crisp and fresh, but there was an underlying current of magic, something almost tangible.

Bharat paused to take it all in. "This place... it's unlike anything I've ever seen," he murmured, running a hand through his dishevelled black hair. His physique, athletic from his years of being on the move as a journalist, allowed him to navigate the forest with ease, but his mind struggled to keep up with the reality around him.

He crouched beside one of the trees, his brown eyes sharp and full of curiosity, scanning the intricacies of the bark. The tree itself seemed alive, not in the ordinary sense of a living organism but in a way that felt conscious, as though it was watching him as much as he was observing it. Bharat ran his fingers over the surface of the tree, feeling the smoothness beneath the rough exterior, and a gentle pulse—a warmth—surged up through his hand. He pulled away quickly, startled.

"What kind of world is this?" he whispered under his breath. The forest, alive and buzzing with a quiet energy, made him feel both small and significant at the same time, as if the world was both welcoming him and testing his resolve.

His thoughts spun back to the ship. "How did I even get here?" Bharat asked himself, frustrated by the lack of clarity. His memories were fragmented—the ship, the strange light, and now this. Nothing made sense, and yet everything felt more real than the life he had known in Mumbai. As a journalist, Bharat thrived on uncovering the unknown, but now the unknown had swallowed him whole, and he was left searching for answers that seemed just out of reach.

As Bharat continued to walk through the forest, the dense trees and the magical glow began to thin out. The rhythmic rustling of leaves was replaced by a faint, rhythmic thumping sound that seemed to vibrate through the ground. Following the sound, Bharat found himself at the edge of a clearing.

What lay before him was a small village, tucked into the forest as if it had grown from the earth itself. The houses were simple but elegant, built from wood and stone. Their roofs were thatched with thick layers of straw, and smoke rose from chimneys, curling into the air. The entire village seemed to breathe in harmony with the land—calm, peaceful, yet brimming with a vitality that Bharat could feel resonating within him.

The villagers moved gracefully around the clearing, their movements fluid as though in perfect synchronisation with the world around them. Bharat was hesitant to step forward, standing just on the edge of the clearing, concealed by the shadows of the trees. These people were unlike anyone he had ever encountered. Their clothes were woven from materials that shimmered faintly in the sunlight, and their eyes seemed to glow with an inner light. Their skin appeared warm, radiant, and almost otherworldly.

Bharat's heart pounded in his chest as he observed them. "Who are these people? Where am I?" His thoughts raced. He was both awestruck and unnerved by their beauty and their apparent connection to this strange world.

Gathering his courage, Bharat took a deep breath and stepped into the clearing. His movements were quiet, but as soon as his foot touched the soft grass, the villagers turned toward him, their eyes curious but not hostile. They regarded him as if he was something rare and unexpected, yet not unwelcome.

One of them, a tall man with long, flowing silver hair and piercing blue eyes, separated from the group and approached Bharat. He wore a robe of deep green, the material rich and fluid, giving him an air of authority. His eyes were kind yet intense, filled with a wisdom that spoke of centuries of experience.

"Welcome, traveller," the man said, his voice smooth, resonant, and calming. "You have journeyed far to reach Aryavrata."

Bharat blinked, momentarily thrown by the man's words. "Aryavrata?" he echoed, the name sounding foreign yet familiar, as though he had heard it in a dream. "Is that where I am?"

The man nodded, his silver hair catching the light as he moved. "Indeed. You have crossed into a land beyond your own."

Bharat's heart raced, his mind struggling to catch up. "How did I get here?" he asked, the memories of the ship and the glowing light flashing through his mind. "I was on a ship... There was this light, and then—"

The man's lips curled into a knowing smile. "The ship was your vessel, a bridge between your world and ours. The light was the gateway. You were guided here, Bharat."

The man spoke his name with such familiarity that Bharat felt both disoriented and oddly comforted. "Guided?" Bharat's voice wavered with uncertainty. "But why me?"

"You have been chosen," the man said, his tone gentle but firm. "There is much you do not yet understand, but in time, all will become clear. For now, you must come with me. There are those who have awaited your arrival."

Bharat hesitated, feeling a strange mixture of fear and intrigue. His instincts told him to trust this man, but his journalist's mind screamed for more answers, more facts. Still, with no other choice and an undeniable pull toward whatever lay ahead, Bharat nodded and followed.

The man led Bharat through the village, where the villagers watched him with a reverence that made Bharat uncomfortable. They whispered among themselves in soft voices, too low for him to understand, but he could feel their eyes on him, studying him as if he were some kind of enigma.

As they walked, Bharat took in the details of the village. The houses, though simple, were beautifully constructed with an earthy elegance that blended into the natural surroundings. Each one was unique, adorned with carvings of strange symbols and designs that seemed to tell stories of ancient times. The pathways were lined with flowers that bloomed in brilliant, otherworldly colours—hues Bharat had never seen before. The air was sweet with the scent of those flowers, mingled with the warm smell of burning wood from the chimneys.

Finally, they reached the heart of the village, where a large, ornate building stood. It was unlike the other structures—grander, more imposing. The walls were made of smooth stone, adorned with intricate carvings of symbols that seemed to shimmer in the fading light. Two large statues flanked the entrance, each depicting a warrior holding a sword and shield, their expressions fierce and resolute. The building radiated a sense of power and knowledge, as if it held the secrets of the universe within its walls.

"This is the Hall of Knowledge," the man explained, gesturing toward the grand structure. "It is where we gather to share wisdom, learn from the past, and prepare for the future."

Bharat's breath caught in his throat. The Hall of Knowledge seemed to pulse with energy, as if it were alive, breathing with the knowledge of countless generations. The carvings on the walls seemed to move, shifting subtly as if the stories they depicted were still unfolding. Bharat felt a shiver run down his spine as he approached the entrance.

As they stepped inside, Bharat was struck by the sheer size and grandeur of the hall. The ceiling stretched high above, supported by massive pillars that were carved with intricate designs. The walls were lined with shelves, each filled with ancient books, scrolls, and artifacts, all meticulously preserved. In the centre of the hall stood a large table, around which several people were gathered, their faces serious and intent as they studied the objects before them.

One of them, an elderly man with a long white beard and eyes that sparkled with wisdom, looked up as Bharat and his guide entered. His presence was commanding, yet there was a warmth in his gaze that put Bharat at ease.

"Ah, you have brought our guest," the old man said, his voice warm and welcoming. "Welcome to Aryavrata, Bharat. We have been expecting you."

Bharat blinked, surprised. "You... you know my name?"

The old man chuckled softly, his beard quivering with the motion. "We know much about you, young one. You have been foretold in our prophecies, the one who would come from another world to aid us in our time of need."

Bharat felt a wave of disbelief wash over him. "Prophecies? I'm just a journalist... I'm not some kind of saviour."

The old man's expression softened, and he stepped closer, resting a reassuring hand on Bharat's shoulder. "You may not see it yet, Bharat, but your arrival here is not by chance. You have a role to play in the events to come, a role that only you can fulfill."

Bharat swallowed hard, feeling the weight of the old man's words settle on his shoulders. The idea of being part of some grand prophecy was overwhelming, and yet, deep down, he felt a strange sense of inevitability. "What am I supposed to do?" he asked, his voice barely more than a whisper.

"There is much to discuss, and you will need time to process it all," the old man replied kindly. "But first, there are others you must meet. They will help guide you on your journey."

The man who had led Bharat through the village stepped forward, placing a hand on the elder's shoulder. "Allow me to introduce myself," he said. "I am Shivdutt, the chief elder of Aryavrata."

Up close, Bharat could see Shivdutt's silver hair, which gleamed like polished metal in the light of the hall. His eyes were piercing, the kind that seemed to look straight through a person and into their soul. His presence was both commanding and comforting, as though he carried the weight of leadership with ease, but with the care of a father.

Shivdutt spoke with a wisdom that only came from centuries of guiding others. His words were carefully chosen, and his tone was calm, unhurried. Bharat felt an inexplicable sense of trust toward him, though he had only just met him.

"It was I who saw the signs of your arrival," Shivdutt continued. "And it is my duty to ensure you are prepared for the task ahead."

Bharat nodded slowly, still trying to wrap his mind around everything he was being told. "I appreciate the welcome," he began, his voice shaky, "but I'm still not sure what's happening, or what I'm supposed to do."

Shivdutt smiled kindly, his intense eyes softening just a little. "You will soon understand, Bharat. But for now, let me introduce you to those who will accompany you on your journey."

As if on cue, two figures stepped forward from the shadows at the back of the hall.

The first was a woman, tall and strong, with sharp features and piercing green eyes that glowed with fierce intensity. She was dressed in gleaming armour, her posture radiating confidence and power. Every movement she made was precise and calculated, as though she were always ready for battle. Her dark hair was tied back in a loose braid, and the armour she wore clinked faintly as she moved.

"This is Riya," Shivdutt said, gesturing to the warrior. "She is one of Aryavrata's finest warriors, known for her skill in combat and her unwavering dedication to protecting our land."

Riya's gaze locked onto Bharat's, her eyes assessing him with an intensity that made him feel both scrutinised and judged. She had the bearing of someone who had seen countless battles and emerged victorious. Her armour bore the marks of many fights—scratches and dents that told the story of her resilience.

"You don't look like much of a fighter," she said bluntly, her voice hard but not unkind. "But if the elders believe you're the one from the prophecy, then I'm willing to give you a chance. Just don't expect me to go easy on you."

Bharat was taken aback by her directness but managed to nod. "I'll do my best," he replied, trying to sound confident despite the nerves tightening in his stomach. He knew he wasn't a warrior, but something about Riya's words made him want to prove himself.

Shivdutt then turned to the second figure, a young man who stood beside Riya with a quiet, composed demeanour. He was shorter than her, with a more relaxed posture, but there was an air of intelligence about him that was unmistakable. His eyes were sharp, gleaming with a thoughtful intensity, and his features were calm, almost serene.

"And this is Aarav," Shivdutt continued. "Aarav is one of our most knowledgeable scholars. He has spent his life studying the ancient texts and prophecies of Aryavrata."

Aarav smiled faintly and inclined his head in greeting. His presence was calming, a stark contrast to Riya's intensity. "Don't worry, Bharat," he said, his voice soft and reassuring. "I'm not as intimidating as Riya here. I'm more interested in solving puzzles than fighting battles. But make no mistake—what lies ahead will challenge us all in ways we can't yet imagine."

Bharat felt a wave of relief at Aarav's words. Unlike Riya, Aarav didn't seem to expect Bharat to be a warrior or a leader. His calm demeanour made Bharat feel like he wasn't alone in facing the challenges ahead.

"I'm glad to have you both with me," Bharat said honestly. "I have no idea what I'm supposed to do, but I'm willing to learn."

Riya's expression softened slightly, though her tone remained firm. "We'll see what you're made of soon enough," she said. "The road ahead isn't easy, and there's no room for hesitation. If you're going to be our leader, you'll need to prove you have what it takes."

Aarav nodded in agreement. "Riya's right," he said, his voice thoughtful. "The challenges we face won't just be physical. They'll test your mind and spirit as well. But don't worry, we're here to help you every step of the way."

As Bharat looked at the three of them—Shivdutt, Riya, and Aarav—he felt a strange mix of emotions. Awe at the power and wisdom they exuded, anxiety over the unknown challenges that awaited, and a growing determination to prove himself worthy of the trust they were placing in him. These were not ordinary people; they were warriors and scholars of a world far beyond anything Bharat had ever imagined, and they believed in him.

For a moment, Bharat wondered why—why had he been chosen? What made him, a simple journalist, worthy of their trust? But as he looked into their eyes—Shivdutt's steady gaze, Riya's fierce determination, and Aarav's quiet confidence—he realised that he might never fully understand. What mattered now was that they were counting on him, and he couldn't let them down.

"Thank you," Bharat said, his voice steady, despite the storm of emotions swirling inside him. "I don't know what lies ahead, but I'll do whatever it takes to help."

Shivdutt nodded approvingly, his eyes gleaming with a mixture of pride and reassurance. "That is all we can ask for, Bharat. Now, let us sit and discuss what lies ahead. The road will not be easy, and there is much you need to understand before we begin."

As they sat down at the large table, Bharat couldn't shake the feeling of destiny settling over him. This world, this quest—it was far beyond anything he had ever imagined. But as he looked around at the faces of those who believed in him, he knew deep down that he was exactly where he was meant to be.

And so, the journey began.

CHAPTER V

The Prophecy Unfolds

The Hall of Knowledge buzzed with a quiet energy as Bharat, Riya, Aarav, and Shivdutt gathered around the large stone table. The room was bathed in the warm glow of the suspended lamps, their soft light flickering and casting long, distorted shadows on the walls adorned with ancient carvings. These carvings, intricate and detailed, told the story of Aryavrata's creation, the rise of its greatest heroes, and the tragedies that had befallen the realm over millennia. Bharat couldn't help but run his eyes over them, taking in the depictions of battles fought, lives sacrificed, and, most importantly, the balance that had always been maintained between light and darkness in this mysterious world. Each etched image seemed to shimmer faintly, as though holding a secret that was just out of reach.

The hall itself was grander than anything Bharat had ever seen, more majestic even than the ancient temples he had visited as a journalist in India. Its high ceilings were supported by enormous stone pillars, each carved with symbols that Bharat couldn't yet decipher but felt their weight. The air inside was cool, a contrast to the humid warmth outside, and carried a faint scent of ancient parchment, wood, and something else—a deep, earthy aroma that spoke of age and wisdom. Everything about this place made Bharat feel small and yet, at the same time, connected to something infinitely larger. Here, in the Hall of Knowledge, he wasn't just a man from Mumbai—he was part of Aryavrata's history now.

As Bharat sat at the table, surrounded by the weight of so much knowledge and history, he felt a mixture of awe and anxiety. This wasn't just another mission for his career; this was about life and death—about the fate of an entire world. His heart pounded in his chest, and for the first time, he wondered if he was truly up to the task. He could feel the pressure of Shivdutt's gaze, the eyes of a man who had lived through centuries of wisdom and battle. Bharat knew that Shivdutt had seen more than any mortal man could comprehend, and yet here he was, placing his faith in Bharat—a mere human.

Shivdutt's eyes, sharp and full of wisdom, regarded Bharat with a mixture of warmth and gravity. His presence was commanding, not just because of his tall, lean frame but because of the aura of authority that clung to him like a cloak. His long silver hair flowed down his back, a stark contrast to the deep green robe embroidered with golden symbols he wore. Each step he took seemed to echo through the hall, resonating with the weight of the decisions he had to make as the chief elder of Aryavrata. There was something ethereal about Shivdutt, something almost divine. His piercing blue eyes seemed to see through Bharat, as though they could peer into his very soul and weigh his worth.

"Bharat," Shivdutt began, his voice calm but carrying a weight that immediately demanded attention. "What you have stepped into is far more than just a journey across worlds. Aryavrata has been at peace for many generations, but that peace is now threatened by a force older and darker than most can comprehend."

Bharat's hands trembled slightly as he clenched them into fists, trying to steady himself. His mind buzzed with questions, but he kept his mouth shut, waiting for more.

The elder's words carried an eerie finality, as though what he was about to reveal would change everything Bharat thought he knew about the world.

Before Bharat could respond, Aarav spoke, his voice calm but filled with an unspoken urgency. Aarav's demeanour was quieter than the others, more reserved, but there was a sharpness in his intelligence that could not be ignored. His dark hair, neatly combed, framed his angular face, giving him an almost scholarly appearance. Despite being younger than the others in the room, there was an ancient quality to Aarav, as though he had spent years poring over texts that had long since turned to dust.

"The one behind this threat is a sorcerer known as Raktashak," Aarav said, his tone sombre. His words were measured, as though each one carried the weight of a thousand years of history. "His name is spoken with fear throughout Aryavrata, for he once served as a guardian of this realm, only to be corrupted by his desire for ultimate power."

Bharat's curiosity was piqued, but so was his anxiety. "Raktashak... What does he want?" His voice was low, as though speaking the sorcerer's name aloud might summon him.

Riya, who had been standing silently with her arms crossed, stepped forward, her expression hardening. Her piercing green eyes, which had initially scrutinised Bharat with skepticism, now glowed with intensity. She was a vision of strength and precision, her tall, muscular frame covered in sleek armour that gleamed under the lamplight. Every inch of her exuded confidence, the kind that only came from years of battle and surviving against the odds. The sword strapped to her back was not just a weapon; it was an extension of her, a symbol of the warrior she had become.

"He seeks the Sankalp Shila," Riya said, her voice cold and steady. "A stone of unimaginable power that holds the fate of Aryavrata within it. If Raktashak were to gain control of the stone, he could bend its power to his will, plunging Aryavrata into eternal darkness."

Her words hit Bharat like a punch to the gut. He had expected danger, but this... this was something else entirely. The thought of a single stone holding so much power, capable of changing the entire course of a world, made his head spin. Bharat's throat went dry as he asked, "And this Sankalp Shila... what is it exactly?"

Shivdutt stepped forward, his voice filled with reverence. "The Sankalp Shila is no ordinary stone. It is said to be a creation of the gods, forged at the beginning of time to maintain the balance between light and darkness, order and chaos. Whoever possesses the Sankalp Shila has the power to either save or destroy Aryavrata."

Bharat's mind raced as he absorbed the information. The weight of responsibility pressed down on him harder than before, as though the air in the hall had become heavier. He could almost feel the immense power of the Sankalp Shila just from Shivdutt's description. His thoughts flickered back to the carvings on the walls—could those be stories of others who had sought the stone? Or perhaps tales of battles fought to protect it?

"And Raktashak... he wants to use the stone to take over Aryavrata?" Bharat asked, his voice quieter now, the enormity of the situation sinking in.

Aarav's eyes darkened, the weight of the truth visible in his gaze. "Yes. If Raktashak gains control of the Sankalp Shila, he will use its power to corrupt the very fabric of this world, creating a realm of despair and suffering. The prophecy states that a warrior from another world will come to Aryavrata in its hour of need, someone who can find the Sankalp Shila before Raktashak and use it to restore balance."

Bharat's stomach churned. His mind was a whirlwind of conflicting thoughts and emotions. He had always been curious, drawn to mysteries, but this—this was too much. Could he really be the one they were looking for? The warrior from another world?

"And you think I'm that warrior?" Bharat's voice cracked slightly as he spoke, the gravity of the situation overwhelming him.

Shivdutt placed a hand on Bharat's shoulder, his touch surprisingly warm and reassuring. "The signs point to you, Bharat. The ship, the mirror, your arrival here—it all aligns with the ancient prophecies. But prophecy alone is not enough. You must choose this path willingly, knowing the dangers and the sacrifices it may demand."

Bharat felt a rush of conflicting emotions—fear, doubt, but also a strange sense of determination building within him. He glanced at Riya, whose eyes were still fixed on him, assessing his every move, and then at Aarav, whose calmness seemed to anchor him. They believed in him, even if he didn't fully believe in himself yet. But deep down, Bharat knew he couldn't turn away from this. This was his chance to do something truly meaningful, something that could save an entire world.

"I'm willing to do whatever it takes," Bharat said, his voice firm, though the uncertainty still churned within him. "But I'll need your help to understand what I'm up against."

Riya's expression softened slightly, though her gaze remained intense. There was a flicker of respect in her eyes now, a hint that she was beginning to trust him. "You've got us, Bharat. We'll make sure you're ready for what's to come. But know this—Raktashak is not to be underestimated. He's powerful, cunning, and ruthless. The journey to find the Sankalp Shila won't be easy, and he'll do everything in his power to stop us."

Her words were laced with warning, but also with a promise that they wouldn't let him face this alone. Bharat felt a surge of gratitude toward her, knowing that having Riya by his side was both a comfort and a necessity. Her fierce determination was palpable, and Bharat knew that if anyone could help him survive what lay ahead, it was her.

Aarav nodded in agreement, his voice steady but filled with a quiet resolve. "We'll face many trials along the way, some of which will test us in ways we can't yet imagine. But we're not alone. The people of Aryavrata are resilient, and many will stand with us in this fight."

Shivdutt moved to a nearby shelf, his long fingers brushing lightly over the spines of several ancient books. Finally, he selected one, its cover worn and its pages yellowed with age. He brought it to the table, laying it down carefully before them. The book was large, bound in dark leather, and the symbols etched into its cover shimmered faintly in the lamplight, as though they held a magic of their own.

"This," Shivdutt said, placing the book before Bharat, "is the Book of Prophecies. It contains the writings of our ancient seers, who foresaw the coming of Raktashak and the arrival of the one who would oppose him. It also holds the key to finding the Sankalp Shila."

Bharat stared at the book, a sense of awe washing over him. The weight of the book seemed almost symbolic, as though it carried the hopes and fears of an entire world within its pages. He could feel the power radiating from it, not just as an object of knowledge, but as a beacon of destiny.

"How will this help us find the stone?" Bharat asked, his voice tinged with wonder.

Shivdutt opened the book carefully, flipping through the pages with a reverence that spoke of its immense significance. "The seers recorded visions of the stone's location, but the writings are cryptic, filled with symbols and riddles. Aarav has spent years studying these texts, and he believes he has deciphered some of the clues. They point to several ancient temples scattered across Aryavrata, each one containing a fragment of the key to the Sankalp Shila's final resting place."

Aarav leaned forward, tracing his finger over one of the pages. His eyes lit up with excitement, and Bharat could sense the scholar's deep passion for knowledge. "The first temple is located deep within the mountains to the north, hidden by a waterfall that shields its entrance. The path is treacherous, and few who have attempted to reach it have returned. But if we can overcome the trials within, we may find the next clue that will lead us closer to the stone."

Bharat studied the symbols on the page, their meanings just out of reach. His mind raced, trying to piece together what this journey would entail. "So, we're going on a treasure hunt, then?" he asked, a small smile tugging at the corners of his mouth despite the seriousness of the situation.

Aarav smiled slightly in return. "In a way, yes. But this is no ordinary treasure. The temples are ancient and protected by powerful magic. The trials within are designed to test those who seek the stone, to ensure that only the worthy can claim it."

Riya's gaze sharpened, her warrior's instincts kicking in. "We'll need to be prepared for anything. The temples are likely guarded by traps, illusions, and possibly even creatures loyal to Raktashak. We'll have to rely on our wits and our strength to survive."

Bharat swallowed, feeling the enormity of their task sinking in deeper. This was not just an expedition—it was a trial that would test every aspect of his being. Yet, despite the fear clawing at him, there was an undercurrent of excitement that bubbled up. He had always been curious about the world's mysteries, and now, he was about to embark on the greatest mystery of all.

He studied the faces of the three people before him—people who had become his companions in this strange world. Shivdutt's presence was commanding but gentle, like a guiding star that knew exactly where it was leading him. Riya, fierce and determined, was someone Bharat already knew he could trust with his life. Her intensity made him feel both guarded and supported, knowing she would protect him but also push him beyond his limits. And Aarav, with his quiet intellect, felt like an anchor, someone who would always know what to do when the rest of them faltered.

"I'll do whatever it takes," Bharat said, meeting Riya's eyes first. "I know I have a lot to learn, but I won't back down."

Riya's expression softened, just for a moment. "We'll see what you're made of soon enough. The road ahead isn't easy, and there's no room for hesitation. If you're going to be our leader, you'll need to prove you have what it takes."

Aarav nodded in agreement, though his tone was more comforting. "Riya's right. The challenges we face won't be just physical—they'll test your mind and spirit as well. But don't worry, we're here to help you every step of the way."

Bharat felt a wave of gratitude toward them both. Despite the uncertainty, there was a growing sense of camaraderie. He wasn't alone in this. They were a team, bound by fate and circumstance, and together they would face whatever trials lay ahead.

As Shivdutt closed the Book of Prophecies, he looked at Bharat with an expression of deep understanding. "The path ahead is dangerous, Bharat, and there is no guarantee of success. But the fate of Aryavrata rests on your shoulders. If you can find the Sankalp Shila, you will have the power to save this world from Raktashak's darkness. But if you fail..."

He let the sentence hang in the air, the unspoken consequences weighing heavy in the silence that followed. Bharat didn't need to hear the rest. He knew what was at stake.

"I won't fail," Bharat said, his voice steady despite the fear that gnawed at him. "We'll find the Sankalp Shila, and we'll stop Raktashak."

Shivdutt nodded, his expression softening with a hint of pride. "Then it is decided. Tomorrow at dawn, you will begin your journey to the first temple. May the gods watch over you and guide your steps."

As they left the Hall of Knowledge, the weight of what lay ahead settled over Bharat like a heavy cloak. The night was still and cool, the village quiet under the stars, but Bharat felt as though the entire world was holding its breath, waiting for what was to come.

The village, nestled among the towering trees of the forest, looked peaceful and serene in the moonlight. The houses were simple but elegant, made of stone and wood with thatched roofs that gave them a timeless quality.

Smoke curled lazily from the chimneys, and the soft glow of lanterns illuminated the pathways that wound between the homes. It was a village steeped in history, a place where the past and present seemed to coexist in perfect harmony. Bharat could feel the ancient magic that thrummed through the ground beneath his feet, a reminder that this was no ordinary place.

As they walked through the village, Bharat couldn't help but marvel at the beauty of it all. The air was crisp and clean, carrying with it the faint scent of pine and earth. The villagers moved quietly through the streets, their voices low as they whispered among themselves. Some glanced curiously in Bharat's direction, their eyes filled with a mixture of wonder and hope. It was as if they knew who he was—knew that he had come to save them.

"I can't believe how peaceful it is here," Bharat murmured to Aarav as they passed a group of villagers who were gathered around a fire. "It's hard to imagine that a war could be brewing, with everything so calm."

Aarav smiled faintly. "Aryavrata has always been a land of balance, Bharat. But that balance is fragile. It takes only one dark force to upset the equilibrium. That's why we need to act quickly. If Raktashak gains the upper hand, this peace you see now will vanish."

Bharat nodded, understanding the gravity of the situation even more clearly now. He had been given a glimpse of the beauty that Aryavrata had to offer, but he knew that it could all be lost if they failed.

As they approached the edge of the village, the towering structure of the Hall of Knowledge loomed before them once again. It stood like a sentinel at the heart of the village, its stone walls etched with ancient symbols that glowed faintly in the darkness. The hall was a monument to the wisdom and history of Aryavrata, a place where the past was preserved and the future was shaped.

Riya stepped forward, her gaze fixed on the horizon. "We should rest now. Tomorrow will be the first step of a long journey."

Bharat felt a pang of uncertainty as they parted ways for the night. He made his way to the small house that had been prepared for him, its interior simple but comfortable. The bed was covered with soft furs, and a small fire crackled in the hearth, filling the room with warmth. But despite the comfort, Bharat found it hard to relax. His mind was racing with thoughts of the journey ahead, of the responsibilities that had been placed on his shoulders.

He lay on the bed, staring up at the wooden beams above him. The firelight flickered, casting dancing shadows on the walls, but it did little to ease the tension that knotted in his chest. He couldn't shake the feeling that he was being watched, that the weight of Aryavrata's fate was pressing down on him even now.

"What have I gotten myself into?" he whispered to himself, his voice barely audible in the quiet room.

But even as the doubts crept in, there was a flicker of determination within him. He had come this far, and there was no turning back now. He couldn't afford to be afraid—not when so much was at stake.

The night passed slowly, the hours stretching on as Bharat drifted in and out of restless sleep. His dreams were filled with images of the Sankalp Shila, of dark forces gathering on the horizon, and of battles yet to be fought. But through it all, one image stood out—Riya, Aarav, and Shivdutt standing by his side, their faces resolute, their eyes filled with the same determination that burned within him.

When the first light of dawn finally broke through the darkness, Bharat rose from the bed, his body weary but his mind clear. He dressed quickly, gathering the few belongings he had been given, and made his way to the village square, where Riya, Aarav, and Shivdutt were already waiting.

The sky was painted with the soft hues of sunrise, the golden light filtering through the trees and casting long shadows on the ground. The village was quiet, the villagers still asleep, but there was a palpable sense of anticipation in the air. This was the moment they had been waiting for—the beginning of their journey.

Riya greeted Bharat with a nod, her green eyes sharp and focused. She was already dressed for battle, her armour gleaming in the morning light. "Are you ready?" she asked, her voice steady and calm.

Bharat nodded, though his heart pounded in his chest. "As ready as I'll ever be."

Aarav smiled faintly, his calm demeanour a reassuring presence. "Don't worry, Bharat. We've faced worse than this before. We'll get through it."

Shivdutt stepped forward, his expression grave but filled with hope. "Remember, Bharat, this is only the beginning. The path ahead will be difficult, but you are not alone. We are with you, and so is Aryavrata. Trust in yourself, and in the strength of those who stand beside you."

Bharat felt a surge of emotion as he looked at the three people who had become his companions, his allies in this fight. He didn't know what the future held, but he knew one thing for certain—he would fight with everything he had to protect this world.

And so, as the first rays of the sun broke over the horizon, casting Aryavrata in a golden glow, Bharat, Riya and Aarav set out on their journey—a journey that would take them to the farthest reaches of the realm, to the ancient temples hidden in the mountains, and, ultimately, to the heart of the battle against Raktashak.

The Sankalp Shila was out there, waiting to be found. And with it, the power to change the fate of an entire world.

CHAPTER VI

The First Temple

The villagers had gathered to see them off, their faces a mix of hope and concern. It was early morning, and the first rays of dawn pierced through the mist that clung to the village. The stillness of the moment only added to the gravity of the task ahead. Bharat could feel the weight of their gazes—people who believed in him, people who thought he could be the key to saving Aryavrata.

Shivdutt stood at the front, his long silver hair reflecting the pale light, his deep green robes billowing slightly in the cool breeze. He looked regal and imposing, a figure of ancient wisdom and calm strength. His piercing blue eyes held Bharat's for a long moment, and Bharat could feel the weight of responsibility settle over him even more deeply.

"Remember," Shivdutt said, his voice carrying a tone of urgency, "the path to the temple is fraught with danger. Trust in one another and in the guidance of the ancient texts. Raktashak's influence is strong, and he will try to thwart your progress at every turn. Stay vigilant, and do not let fear cloud your judgement."

His words were not just advice—they were a solemn warning. Bharat felt a tight knot form in his chest. He was about to step into something far bigger than he had ever imagined, and there was no turning back now.

Riya, standing next to him, nodded, her expression resolute. The morning light glinted off her new armour, a set forged from the finest materials Aryavrata had to offer. Her silver breastplate was etched with intricate patterns, representing her status as a warrior of high rank. The armour was lightweight but durable, designed for speed and agility in combat. Over her shoulder, a crimson cloak fluttered lightly, fastened by a silver clasp engraved with the sigil of her house. Her dark hair was pulled back tightly, revealing her sharp features—her green eyes gleaming with determination and a fierce readiness for the battles that lay ahead.

"We'll bring back the next piece of the puzzle, Shivdutt. Count on it," Riya said with a calm confidence that only a seasoned warrior could possess.

Aarav stood beside them, adjusting the straps on his satchel filled with scrolls, maps, and supplies. His new robes were a deep forest green, trimmed with delicate gold runes stitched along the sleeves and hem. They were crafted from a special fabric that offered some protection but didn't hinder movement, perfect for someone like Aarav who valued agility and speed of thought. A belt fastened at his waist held several pouches containing potions, herbs, and small tools. Though Aarav lacked the imposing physical presence of Riya, his keen intellect and deep understanding of Aryavrata's ancient knowledge made him an essential part of their team. His calm demeanour was comforting, but Bharat could sense the seriousness behind his eyes.

"I've studied the maps and texts carefully," Aarav said, his voice steady but tinged with caution. "The temple is hidden deep within the mountains, protected by powerful magic. We must be prepared for anything."

Bharat glanced down at himself. He, too, had been given new clothes and gear for the journey ahead. His old, worn shirt and jeans had been replaced with a durable brown tunic made from a sturdy fabric that felt soft but strong. It was simple, yet functional, allowing him to move easily.

Over the tunic, he wore a lightweight leather breastplate that felt foreign on his chest—Bharat had never been a fighter, and the idea of wearing armour still felt strange to him. His boots were new as well, designed for traversing the rough terrain they were about to face. A belt fastened at his waist carried a short sword. He had hesitated when Riya first handed it to him the night before, unsure of his ability to use it effectively, but now it hung there, a constant reminder of the dangers that lay ahead.

I'm just a journalist, Bharat thought to himself, his stomach twisting with a mix of anxiety and disbelief. What am I doing with a sword strapped to my waist?

Yet, there was no turning back now. The responsibility of this journey had fallen on his shoulders, and despite the fear gnawing at him, Bharat was determined to see it through. He knew that the people of Aryavrata were counting on him, and though he wasn't sure how he could live up to their expectations, he wasn't about to let them down.

Shivdutt's gaze softened as he looked at Bharat. "You have come far already, Bharat. Trust in yourself as much as you trust in your companions."

Bharat swallowed hard, nodding. "I'm ready," he said, though his voice held more uncertainty than confidence. The truth was, he wasn't sure if he was ready, but he knew he couldn't back out now. Not with so much at stake.

Riya's hand landed on his shoulder, her grip firm but reassuring. "You're ready," she said, echoing his words but with far more conviction. Her eyes bore into his with a quiet intensity. "We'll face whatever comes together. Just stay sharp, and don't hesitate when it's time to act."

Bharat felt a wave of gratitude for her steady presence. Riya was a warrior through and through—confident, strong, and fearless. She had seen countless battles and knew how to survive in this world. With her and Aarav by his side, Bharat felt a small measure of comfort. They would face the challenges ahead together, as a team.

Aarav adjusted the straps of his satchel one last time, his brow furrowed in concentration. "This is just the beginning, but we're as prepared as we can be," he said quietly, his voice filled with a calm determination.

With a final nod from Shivdutt, the trio set off, leaving the village behind as they ventured into the dense forest. Bharat could hear the faint sounds of the villagers offering their blessings and prayers as they disappeared into the trees. The path ahead of them was narrow, winding through towering trees and thick undergrowth. Sunlight filtered through the leaves, casting dappled shadows on the ground. The forest was alive with the sounds of nature—birdsong, the rustling of leaves, and the distant chirping of insects—but there was an undercurrent of tension that Bharat couldn't shake.

The further they walked, the more the air seemed to change. The once vibrant colours of the forest began to dim, the trees growing taller and denser, their trunks twisting and gnarled like ancient sentinels. The sunlight, which had initially felt warm and welcoming, now struggled to pierce through the thickening canopy, casting long shadows across their path.

"This place... it's incredible," Bharat said softly, his voice filled with awe as he gazed at the towering trees around him. He had never seen anything like it. The trees in Aryavrata were unlike those in his world—massive, ancient things with roots that seemed to stretch into the very core of the earth. Their leaves shimmered faintly in the light, as if touched by magic. Flowers bloomed in a riot of colours, their petals delicate and fragrant, filling the air with their sweet scent.

Riya glanced at him, a small smile tugging at her lips. "Aryavrata is a land of wonders," she said, her voice holding a note of pride. "But it's also a land of great danger. The beauty you see here can quickly turn deadly if you're not careful."

Aarav nodded in agreement, his eyes scanning the forest with a practised eye. "Nature in Aryavrata is powerful and unpredictable. It's what gives this realm its strength, but it also makes it a place where the unprepared don't last long."

Bharat could feel the truth in their words. Despite the breathtaking beauty of the forest, there was an undercurrent of danger lurking beneath the surface. He could sense it in the way the trees seemed to close in around them, in the way the air grew heavier and more oppressive with each step. His hand instinctively rested on the hilt of his sword, though he wasn't entirely sure how much use it would be if something—or someone—decided to attack.

They continued their journey in silence for a while, each of them lost in their own thoughts. Bharat's mind raced with questions and doubts. He had never faced anything like this before. Back in Mumbai, his biggest challenge had been chasing down leads for stories. Now, he was on a quest to save an entire realm from destruction. It all felt so surreal, like something out of a fantasy novel. But this was real—more real than anything he had ever experienced. The weight of it all pressed down on him, making it hard to breathe.

What if I fail? The thought gnawed at him relentlessly, but he pushed it aside. Now was not the time for doubt.

After several hours of walking, the forest finally began to thin out, and they found themselves standing at the base of a towering mountain range. The mountains were massive, their peaks disappearing into the clouds, their slopes steep and treacherous. A waterfall cascaded down from one of the cliffs, its roar echoing through the valley below. The water shimmered with a strange, ethereal light, casting rainbows in the mist that swirled around the base of the waterfall.

"There it is," Aarav said, pointing to a narrow path that wound its way up the mountain. "The entrance to the first temple is hidden behind that waterfall. But getting there won't be easy. The path is steep and unstable, and there are likely traps set to keep out intruders."

Riya adjusted the straps on her armour, her eyes scanning the path ahead with the sharpness of a hawk. "We'll need to be careful. This is where the real test begins."

Bharat stared up at the path, his stomach churning with a mix of excitement and dread. The climb looked daunting, but there was no turning back now. They had come too far to stop.

I have to do this, Bharat reminded himself, steeling his resolve. "Let's go," he said, his voice filled with determination.

The climb was arduous. The path was narrow and treacherous, with loose rocks crumbling beneath their feet, threatening to send them tumbling down the steep slope. Bharat's legs burned with the effort, his muscles straining as they ascended higher and higher. The air grew thinner as they climbed, making each breath a struggle. Sweat trickled down Bharat's brow despite the cold, his heart pounding in his chest.

Riya, leading the way, moved with the grace and agility of a seasoned warrior. Her every step was deliberate, her eyes constantly scanning their surroundings for any sign of danger. Aarav, though not as physically strong, kept pace with an almost quiet determination, his mind always working, calculating their next move.

Bharat struggled to keep up, his lungs burning with the effort. He marvelled at his companions—Riya's strength, Aarav's intelligence. They seemed so sure of themselves, so prepared for the challenges ahead. Bharat, on the other hand, felt like an outsider, a man thrust into a world he didn't fully understand.

What am I doing here? The thought crossed his mind more than once, but he pushed it aside. He had a role to play in this, even if he didn't fully understand what it was yet.

As they neared the waterfall, the mist thickened, drenching them in cold, shimmering droplets. The roar of the water was deafening, making it difficult to communicate. Bharat could barely see a few feet ahead of him, the world around him reduced to a swirling blur of white mist and the deafening sound of rushing water.

Riya, leading the way, suddenly stopped, holding up a hand to signal the others. "Wait," she called out over the noise of the waterfall. "There's something ahead."

Bharat and Aarav moved closer, squinting through the mist. At first, Bharat saw nothing but the churning water, but then he noticed something strange about the way the mist swirled in front of them. It was as if the air itself was shifting, distorting, creating a shimmering barrier.

"It's a magical ward," Aarav said, his voice tinged with both admiration and concern. "A powerful one. It's designed to repel anyone who tries to enter the temple without the proper knowledge or strength."

Riya narrowed her eyes, examining the barrier. "Can we get through it?"

Aarav nodded, though his expression was serious. "Yes, but it won't be easy. We'll need to find the right frequency to disrupt the ward's energy. It's like tuning into the right station on a radio, but with magic."

Bharat's mind raced as he tried to understand what Aarav was saying. "How do we do that?"

Aarav reached into his satchel and pulled out a small, intricately carved stone. "This is a resonance stone," he explained. "It's attuned to the magical frequencies of Aryavrata. If I can find the right frequency, we can disrupt the ward and pass through."

He closed his eyes, holding the stone in both hands, and began to hum softly. The sound was low and steady, resonating in the air around them. Slowly, the stone began to glow, emitting a soft, pulsing light that matched the rhythm of Aarav's hum. The shimmering barrier in front of them began to ripple, the air vibrating with energy. The mist around them seemed to dance in response, swirling in intricate patterns.

It was as if the very fabric of reality was bending to Aarav's will.

Suddenly, the barrier shuddered and then dissipated, the air returning to its normal state. The path to the temple was now clear, the entrance hidden behind the cascading water.

Aarav opened his eyes, the glow from the stone fading. "It's done," he said, a hint of weariness in his voice. "We can go through."

Riya gave a nod of approval. "Well done, Aarav. Let's move."

They carefully stepped through the waterfall, the cold water soaking them to the bone. Beyond the curtain of water, they found themselves standing before a large, intricately carved stone door. The door was adorned with ancient symbols and runes, similar to those Bharat had seen in the Hall of Knowledge.

"This is it," Riya said, her voice hushed with reverence. "The entrance to the first temple."

Aarav examined the carvings, tracing his fingers over the symbols. "These runes are part of the protection spells that guard the temple. They've been here for centuries, maybe even millennia."

As Bharat stood before the entrance of the first temple, his heart raced with anticipation. The towering structure loomed above him, half-hidden behind the cascading waterfall. The mist and water droplets caught in the sunlight, casting shimmering rainbows in the air, adding an ethereal beauty to the already awe-inspiring sight. But beneath that beauty lay a sense of foreboding—a weighty, almost oppressive energy that Bharat could feel pressing down on him.

From where he stood, the temple appeared ancient, its stone facade worn down by centuries of exposure to the elements, yet still imbued with an undeniable sense of power. The architecture was unlike anything Bharat had seen before. It wasn't grand or ornamental in the traditional sense, but rather it possessed a primal majesty that seemed to belong to another age—an age of gods and legends. Massive blocks of stone formed the walls, each one etched with intricate carvings and symbols that seemed to pulse with an inner light, as though the temple itself was alive.

Every inch of the stone was covered in these carvings—runes and sigils that Bharat couldn't even begin to decipher. They twisted and wound their way across the surface, forming patterns that hinted at forgotten histories and long-lost rituals. Some of the figures carved into the walls depicted ancient warriors in battle, while others showed scenes of people gathered in reverence around mystical objects, their faces filled with awe.

What struck Bharat the most was the temple's sheer size. It dwarfed them all, standing like a giant sentinel, guarding the secrets it held within. The entrance, a massive stone door, was set deep into the rock, half-concealed by the waterfall that poured over it. The water crashed down in torrents, but beyond it, Bharat could see the dark, foreboding opening—a mouth leading into the unknown. He felt a chill run down his spine as he stared at the entrance, and he couldn't help but feel as though the temple was watching him in return, waiting for him to step forward.

There was an undeniable sense of age here—an ancient power that had endured for countless generations. It wasn't the kind of decay one would expect from a ruin; rather, it felt like the temple had withstood the passage of time intentionally, a guardian of something far greater than anyone could comprehend. The stone beneath his feet felt solid and eternal, as though it had never known change, as though it had existed since the beginning of time itself.

Despite its rough-hewn appearance, the temple exuded an elegance born from its simplicity. The entrance was flanked by two towering statues, each one depicting an armoured warrior holding a sword and shield. Their faces were stern, their eyes unyielding, as if they had been placed there to judge anyone who dared step beyond the threshold. Bharat felt as though they were staring directly at him, their stone gazes assessing whether he was worthy to enter.

The air around the temple felt different too—thicker, heavier, almost electric. Every breath Bharat took was filled with the energy of the place, a strange mixture of anticipation and dread. The sound of the waterfall crashing against the rocks blended with the low, almost imperceptible hum that seemed to emanate from the temple itself. It was as if the entire structure was alive, resonating with an ancient magic that had been dormant for centuries, waiting for the right moment to awaken.

As Bharat took it all in, he found himself both awed and intimidated. The sheer enormity of the temple made him feel small, insignificant in the grand scheme of things. He was just one man standing before a relic of another world, another time. And yet, despite the fear that gripped his heart, there was also a sense of excitement—a thrill that coursed through his veins as he realised that he was standing on the threshold of something extraordinary.

His fingers brushed against the cold, damp stone as he approached the door. It was slick with moisture from the waterfall, but beneath that, Bharat could feel the raw power humming through it, a faint vibration that sent a shiver down his spine. The runes carved into the surface glowed faintly, casting an eerie light that illuminated the surrounding mist. It was as if the temple was alive, responding to his presence.

Bharat's mind raced as he stared at the door. This was more than just a temple. It was a gateway—a place where the boundaries between worlds blurred. The air itself seemed to ripple with magic, and Bharat could feel it—an ancient force that called to him, urging him forward. Yet, there was also a warning in that call, a sense that the temple would not easily yield its secrets. The trials that awaited inside would be unlike anything he had faced before.

The sense of history and destiny hung heavy in the air. Bharat knew this temple had been waiting for him, for them. The thought filled him with equal parts excitement and trepidation. Whatever lay inside would test them, not just physically, but in ways that went far deeper—ways he was not sure he was prepared for.

As he stood there, his heart pounding in his chest, Bharat knew that beyond this door lay the next step in their journey. The path to the Sankalp Shila started here, and with it, the fate of Aryavrata rested on his shoulders.

With one last glance at his companions—Riya, standing tall and resolute, and Aarav, his mind already working through the puzzles they would face—Bharat took a deep breath and stepped forward toward the temple door, ready to face whatever awaited them inside.

Bharat stared at the door, a sense of awe and trepidation washing over him. This was the first real step toward the Sankalp Shila, and it felt like the weight of history was pressing down on him.

"What do we do now?" Bharat asked, his voice barely above a whisper.

Aarav looked at him, his expression serious. "Now, we face the trials within. The temple will test us—our strength, our resolve, our very souls. If we pass, we'll find the next clue that will lead us to the Sankalp Shila. If we fail..."

He didn't need to finish the sentence. The consequences were clear.

With a deep breath, Riya stepped forward and pushed against the stone door. It groaned in protest, but slowly, it began to move, opening to reveal a dark passageway that led deep into the heart of the mountain.

CHAPTER VII

The Trials

The air inside was cold and still, and the darkness clung to them like a suffocating cloak. Bharat felt a chill run down his spine as they stepped inside, the stone door behind them sealing with a heavy, echoing thud. For a moment, they were plunged into total blackness, and it was as if the temple itself had swallowed them whole.

Bharat's heart raced. His breathing quickened, the oppressive atmosphere pressing down on him like an invisible weight. The torchlight that Riya ignited flickered weakly, barely illuminating the narrow passage ahead of them. The walls, lined with intricate carvings of ancient battles, rituals, and shadowy figures, seemed to shift and twist in the dim light, as though the very temple were alive and watching them.

"Stay close," Riya whispered, her voice low but resolute.

Bharat nodded, though a knot of unease tightened in his chest. Something felt wrong—unnatural. It was as if the air itself was watching them, waiting for them to make a mistake. The sense of foreboding grew heavier with each step, and Bharat couldn't shake the feeling that they were being stalked by unseen eyes, that the temple itself was testing their resolve from the moment they stepped through the door.

The further they walked, the colder it became, and the weight of silence pressed on them, broken only by the occasional drip of water echoing somewhere in the distance. Every shadow, every movement of the torch's flame, felt like a potential threat. Bharat's fingers itched for a weapon, but he knew that here, in this ancient place, physical strength alone would not be enough.

Finally, after what felt like hours of walking through the suffocating dark, they emerged into a vast chamber. Bharat's breath caught in his throat as his eyes adjusted to the expanse before them. The ceiling soared high above, lost in the darkness. Massive stone columns lined the room, their surfaces etched with runes and symbols glowing faintly, casting an eerie light on the floor below.

At the centre of the chamber stood a massive stone pedestal. Upon it rested an artifact—a large, ornately carved stone disk, its surface shimmering with a strange, otherworldly light. The runes carved into it seemed alive, pulsing faintly, as though drawing power from the temple itself.

Bharat's skin prickled with anticipation. There was something ancient and powerful about this place, something that made his heart beat faster with both awe and fear.

"This must be the first trial," Riya said, her voice echoing in the cavernous room. She stepped forward cautiously, her hand resting on the hilt of her sword, eyes scanning the shadows.

Aarav approached the pedestal, his eyes sharp and calculating. "This is no ordinary puzzle," he said softly, as though afraid to disturb the chamber's quiet. His fingers traced the glowing runes on the stone disk. "The runes are from an ancient language—one that predates even the oldest texts in Aryavrata."

Bharat stepped closer, feeling the weight of the temple's gaze on him. "So, how do we solve it?"

Aarav pulled a scroll from his satchel and unrolled it carefully, scanning the ancient symbols etched on the parchment. "These runes represent values—strength, wisdom, sacrifice—but we need to align them in the correct order to unlock the temple's secrets."

Riya frowned, glancing at the looming shadows that filled the chamber. "And if we get it wrong?"

Aarav's expression was grim. "The temple will respond. Likely with a trap or worse."

Bharat swallowed hard, his mind racing. He had never been one for ancient languages or puzzles. He was used to relying on instinct and action. But this... this was different. The temple wasn't testing their ability to fight—it was testing their minds, their teamwork, their resolve.

"We need to think beyond the symbols," Bharat said slowly, trying to understand the logic behind the trial. "This place isn't just testing our knowledge—it's testing our unity. We need to work together, combining our strengths."

Aarav nodded thoughtfully. "Exactly. This trial is about more than just reading ancient runes. It's about understanding the deeper meaning behind them."

The trio worked in silence, the weight of the temple pressing down on them. Bharat watched as Aarav deciphered the runes, his sharp mind piecing together the ancient language, while Riya kept a vigilant eye on the shifting shadows, ready to defend them if the temple's guardians awoke. The tension in the room was palpable, every movement filled with the fear that one wrong symbol could trigger their downfall.

Bharat focused on the patterns in the symbols, looking for connections, for clues in the temple's design that might help them. His instincts, honed from years of journalistic investigation, began to kick in. Slowly, they aligned the symbols, the glowing runes shifting and clicking into place.

Finally, the last symbol slid into position with a satisfying click. The room filled with a soft, pulsing light, and the stone pedestal began to hum with energy. The floor trembled beneath them, and the walls of the chamber shifted, revealing a new passageway. The temple had accepted their solution—for now.

"We did it," Bharat breathed, relief flooding through him.

Aarav nodded, though his expression remained tense. "This is only the beginning."

They pressed forward into the newly revealed passage, the air growing colder and more oppressive with each step. Bharat couldn't shake the feeling that the temple was alive, that it was watching their every move, waiting for them to falter.

The passage led them into another chamber, smaller than the first but no less intimidating. The walls were lined with rows of stone statues, warriors in armour, their expressions fierce and unyielding. The statues felt more like sentinels, watching over the room, waiting to pass judgement.

At the centre of the room stood a stone altar, and upon it rested a gleaming sword. The blade was etched with the same dark runes they had seen before, but these felt different—more ominous, more dangerous.

Aarav's voice was barely a whisper. "This is the second trial—the Trial of Courage."

Riya stepped forward, her eyes narrowing as she studied the sword. "What do we have to do?"

Aarav's gaze swept across the stone warriors. "These statues represent the temple's guardians. One of us must take the sword and face them in combat. It's a test of bravery, of strength. If we fail, the guardians will attack."

Bharat felt a surge of adrenaline. His hands clenched into fists, his mind racing. He wasn't a warrior. He wasn't made for this kind of test. But before he could speak, Riya stepped forward, her expression resolute.

"I'll do it," she said, her voice calm and steady. Without hesitation, she grasped the hilt of the sword and lifted it from the altar.

The moment the sword left the altar, the chamber erupted in sound. The statues around them began to stir, the grinding of stone filling the air as the guardians came to life. Their stone eyes glowed with a cold, menacing light as they raised their weapons and advanced on Riya.

"Get ready," Riya said, her voice unwavering, though her knuckles whitened around the sword's hilt. "This won't be easy."

Bharat's heart pounded in his chest as the first guardian lunged at Riya. Its massive stone body moved with terrifying speed, its sword arcing through the air toward her. Riya met the blow with her own sword, the clash of stone and steel reverberating through the chamber like thunder.

Riya's movements were fast and precise, but the sheer strength of the guardians was overwhelming. Every time she blocked a strike, the force of the impact shook the ground beneath them. Bharat could only watch, his muscles tensing with every swing of the guardian's sword.

Despite the odds, Riya didn't waver. She fought with a grace and ferocity that left Bharat in awe. Each strike of her sword was calculated, each movement deliberate. But the guardians were relentless, their stone forms towering over her as they pressed their assault.

"She can't keep this up forever," Bharat muttered, fear gnawing at him. But interfering would only make things worse.

Riya's breath came in gasps, sweat beading on her brow. But she was a warrior, and warriors didn't back down. She feinted left, then swung her sword in a powerful arc, shattering the blade of the first guardian. The stone warrior faltered, its glowing eyes dimming as it knelt before her, acknowledging defeat.

The other guardians remained still, their challenge met.

Riya lowered her sword, her chest heaving with exhaustion. "It's done," she said, her voice tinged with both relief and weariness.

Aarav approached cautiously, his eyes filled with admiration. "You've proven your courage, Riya. The temple will allow us to pass."

Bharat let out a breath he hadn't realised he was holding. "That was incredible," he said, his voice filled with pride for his companion.

Riya offered him a tired smile. "It's not over yet, Bharat. The hardest trial is still to come."

They moved through the next passageway, the air growing colder and darker as they descended deeper into the temple. The final chamber was unlike anything they had seen. The oppressive energy in the room was palpable, and the walls pulsed with a dark, foreboding light. At the centre of the chamber lay a vast, still pool of dark water, its surface smooth and unbroken.

"What is this place?" Bharat whispered, the words barely leaving his lips.

Aarav's face was drawn, his voice heavy with trepidation. "This is the Trial of the Shadow Realm. The final test."

Riya approached the edge of the pool, her gaze hard and unyielding. "What do we have to do?"

Aarav's eyes remained fixed on the water, his expression dark. "The Shadow Realm brings your inner demons to life. Your fears, your doubts, your regrets—they all take shape in the water. To pass this trial, each of us must confront the darkness within ourselves."

Bharat's skin crawled at the thought. "And if we fail?"

Aarav's voice was grim. "The darkness will consume us."

There was no more time for hesitation. With a deep breath, the three of them stepped into the dark water. Cold seeped into their bones as they waded deeper, the darkness closing in around them, swallowing them whole.

The silence was suffocating. Bharat felt the weight of the water pressing down on him, disorienting him, making it difficult to think. His heart pounded in his chest, and for a moment, he wasn't sure if he could make it.

Then the darkness shifted, and suddenly Bharat was no longer in the temple. He was standing in his childhood home, the warm and comforting surroundings a stark contrast to the cold, oppressive dark he had just left. But something wasn't right. The air was thick with tension, and shadows lurked at the edges of his vision.

As he looked around, he realised he was alone. The house, once filled with laughter and life, was now silent and empty. The dread that washed over him was immediate and overwhelming.

A figure stepped out from the shadows, twisted and distorted, its face a cruel mirror of his own. "You don't belong here," the shadow hissed, its voice echoing with malice. "You're just a scared little boy, lost and alone. You'll never be good enough. Never strong enough to save anyone."

Bharat's chest tightened. The words cut deep. He felt the fear, the doubt rising within him. Was this what he had always feared? That he wasn't enough?

But no. He wouldn't give in to the darkness. Not here, not now.

"No," Bharat said, his voice trembling but firm. "I may be afraid, but I'm not alone. I have people who believe in me, who are counting on me. I won't let you—or anyone else—take that away from me."

The shadow laughed, its form shifting and twisting. "You're weak, Bharat. You can't even save yourself."

Bharat's resolve hardened. He clenched his fists, stepping forward to confront the twisted version of himself. "I'm not weak," he said, his voice growing stronger. "I'm stronger than you think. I'm not perfect, but I'll fight. I'll face whatever comes, and I'll do it with everything I have."

The shadow snarled and lunged at him, its form unravelling as it tried to overpower him. But Bharat didn't flinch. He reached out, embracing the darkness, confronting it head-on.

The shadow screamed, its form dissolving into the air, and suddenly the oppressive weight lifted. Bharat blinked, finding himself back in the temple, the dark energy of the Shadow Realm dissipating.

Riya and Aarav stood nearby, their faces pale, but they too had emerged victorious from their trials. Their expressions were weary, but they had made it through. They had faced their own demons and emerged stronger.

"It's done," Aarav said, his voice filled with relief. "We've passed the final trial."

Bharat nodded, his heart still pounding, but a sense of accomplishment settling over him. "We did it."

As the darkness lifted, the chamber's walls began to glow with a soft, golden light. Etched into the stone, the final clue to the Sankalp Shila's location appeared before them, shimmering like a beacon.

Aarav studied the symbols, his eyes lighting up with understanding. "This is it—the next step in our journey."

Riya sheathed her sword, her expression determined but filled with relief. "We've come this far. We'll see it through to the end."

Bharat felt a sense of unity with his companions, a bond forged in the fire of the temple's trials. "Let's finish this."

With renewed determination, they left the temple, the sunlight warming their faces as they stepped back into the world. The trials had tested their courage, their strength, and their souls, but they had emerged stronger, ready to face whatever awaited them.

The Sankalp Shila was closer than ever, and with it, the power to save Aryavrata.

CHAPTER VIII

Raktashak

The sun dipped low on the horizon, casting long, eerie shadows across the rugged landscape as Bharat, Riya, and Aarav continued their journey. The golden warmth of daylight was slowly being consumed by an unsettling twilight, the air growing colder with each passing moment. The forest that had once teemed with life now felt suffocating, the trees looming like ancient sentinels, their branches twisting together to form a dense, tangled canopy, creating a claustrophobic tunnel around them.

Bharat's heart beat faster with every step, his breath shallow as he struggled to suppress the growing sense of dread building inside him. It wasn't just the ominous darkness that unnerved him—it was the unnatural quiet that seemed to echo in the air. The once-vibrant sounds of birds and rustling leaves were now absent, replaced by an oppressive silence that pressed down on them like a physical force. Even the wind had died, leaving the forest in an unnatural stillness.

"We're getting closer," Aarav said, breaking the silence that had settled over the group. His voice was low, tense, as if afraid to disturb whatever lay ahead. He clutched the ancient map, its edges frayed from years of wear, his brow furrowed as he glanced at it once more. "The path to the next temple should be just beyond this ridge."

Bharat nodded, but his gaze remained fixed on the darkening trail ahead. His muscles ached from the journey, and his body screamed for rest, but he knew there was no time to stop. The trials of the first temple had tested their resolve, but this—this was something different. The air here felt thick with dark magic, and Bharat couldn't shake the feeling that the real challenge was yet to come.

Riya, always vigilant, walked a few steps ahead of them, her hand resting on the hilt of her sword. Her sharp green eyes scanned the area with the precision of a warrior, every muscle in her body tense and ready for battle. "Stay alert," she whispered, her voice barely audible above the eerie silence. "This place doesn't feel right. The darkness here... it's unnatural."

Bharat couldn't agree more. The once-vibrant colours of Aryavrata had faded into a palette of muted greys and blacks. The leaves, once green and full of life, now seemed to hang limp from the trees like wilted corpses. The air, which had been warm and filled with the scent of flowers, now smelled of damp earth and decay. It felt like they had stepped into a place where the light itself was afraid to venture.

His unease only grew as they began to climb the ridge. The trees seemed to press in closer, their gnarled branches forming a twisted lattice overhead, blocking out the last remnants of daylight. The trail beneath their feet became rough and treacherous, each step requiring careful navigation over jagged rocks and hidden roots that seemed to reach out and trip them up.

"We should be nearing the temple," Aarav said, though there was a hint of doubt in his voice. He studied the map with growing concern, his brow furrowed. "But... this doesn't make sense. According to the map, there should be a clearing here, but all I see are these trees."

Riya's expression hardened as she glanced around the dense, unwelcoming foliage. "The map is ancient. Maybe the landscape has changed over the years."

Bharat felt a shiver crawl down his spine, and his voice was barely a whisper as he spoke. "Or maybe it's something else. Something meant to keep us from finding the temple."

Aarav looked up, his eyes meeting Bharat's. A grim realisation settled over him. "You might be right. The closer we get to the temple, the stronger Raktashak's influence becomes. He doesn't want us to succeed. He'll do whatever it takes to stop us."

The mention of Raktashak's name sent a ripple of fear through the group. Though they had yet to face him directly, the stories of his cruelty and dark magic weighed heavily on their minds. The darkness that surrounded them now felt like a manifestation of his will, a silent warning of the danger that awaited them.

"We need to keep moving," Riya said, her voice resolute. "Standing here won't get us anywhere. We'll find a way through this."

With renewed determination, they pressed on. The path became more difficult with each step, the trees seeming to close in around them. Their twisted branches reached out like skeletal fingers, clawing at their clothes and skin. The air grew colder still, so cold that each breath came out in a visible puff of mist. The silence felt oppressive now, as if the very forest were holding its breath, waiting for something terrible to happen.

Bharat's heart pounded in his chest. The sense of dread gnawed at him, growing stronger with every step. He could feel it in his bones—something was watching them. The darkness felt alive, like a sentient being lurking just out of sight, waiting for the right moment to strike.

And then, without warning, the ground beneath them gave way.

Bharat felt the earth shift beneath his feet, and before he could react, he was tumbling down a steep slope. The world spun around him in a blur of shadow and motion as he fell, the sharp rocks and roots tearing at his skin. He hit the ground hard, the impact knocking the breath from his lungs. For a moment, he lay still, dazed and disoriented, the cold earth pressing against his body.

"Bharat! Are you okay?" Riya's voice, sharp with concern, echoed through the darkness.

"I'm fine," Bharat groaned, pushing himself up on his hands and knees. Pain shot through his limbs, but nothing seemed broken. He forced himself to his feet, wincing as he tried to shake off the aches from the fall. "What happened?"

Aarav scrambled down the slope after him, his eyes wide with fear. "The ground... it just collapsed. Like it was waiting for us." He glanced around, his face pale. "This place... it's a trap."

Riya helped Bharat to his feet, her grip strong and reassuring. "We need to be more careful. This place is dangerous, and it's only going to get worse."

Bharat nodded, but his heart raced with growing anxiety. As they surveyed their new surroundings, they realised they had fallen into a deep ravine. The jagged walls rose high on either side, steep and impossible to climb. Shadows clung to the rocky surface like malevolent spirits, and the air was thick with a sense of foreboding.

"This wasn't on the map," Aarav said, frustration creeping into his voice as he clutched the scroll tighter.

"No, this isn't a mistake," Riya said, her voice low. "This is a trap."

Bharat's skin prickled with unease. The darkness here was different—denser, more oppressive. It was as if the very air around them had thickened, and breathing had become a struggle. The sensation of being watched had only intensified. Bharat could feel it like a weight on his chest, a cold gaze that followed their every movement.

"We need to find a way out of here," Riya said, her voice calm but urgent. "We're sitting ducks down here. The longer we stay, the more vulnerable we are."

They began searching for an exit, but every path they tried seemed to lead them deeper into the labyrinthine ravine. The oppressive darkness closed in around them, distorting their sense of direction. It felt as though the very ground beneath their feet was shifting, warping into a nightmare designed to keep them lost.

"This isn't right," Aarav muttered, his voice tinged with frustration and fear. "It's like the ravine is changing, twisting every time we try to move."

Bharat's heart pounded. His instincts screamed that they were being hunted. "It's Raktashak. He's here. He's doing this. He's trying to trap us."

A low, menacing laugh echoed through the ravine, sending a chill down Bharat's spine. The sound was cold and mocking, filled with malice and dark amusement. It reverberated off the walls, surrounding them, making it impossible to pinpoint its source.

"Who's there?" Riya demanded, drawing her sword. Her voice was sharp, though there was a flicker of unease in her eyes.

The laughter grew louder, more menacing. "So, you've finally come," a voice hissed, low and guttural, dripping with venom. "The ones who think they can challenge me, who think they can save Aryavrata."

Bharat's blood ran cold. The voice was unlike anything he had ever heard. It was ancient, filled with malice and cruelty, as if the very air itself was poisoned by its presence.

And then he realised—this was Raktashak.

"Show yourself!" Riya shouted, her eyes scanning the darkness, her sword raised.

The shadows around them began to shift, swirling and coiling like living creatures. And then, from the heart of the darkness, a figure began to materialise. Raktashak.

Bharat's heart nearly stopped as the sorcerer took form. Raktashak was tall, impossibly tall, his body shrouded in a cloak of swirling black mist that seemed to devour the light around him. His eyes were twin orbs of sickly green light, glowing with an unnatural intensity. His face was gaunt and twisted, his lips curled into a cruel, mocking smile that sent shivers down Bharat's spine.

"You think you can defy me?" Raktashak sneered, his voice a whisper that cut through the air like a blade. "You are nothing. Insects scurrying in the dark, desperate to escape your fate."

Bharat's body froze, a cold wave of fear washing over him. He had never felt anything like it before—this presence, this raw, unyielding power. It wasn't just Raktashak's appearance that terrified him—it was the overwhelming sense of dread that radiated from him. The darkness that clung to the sorcerer seemed alive, writhing and twisting as if eager to consume them.

"We're not afraid of you, Raktashak," Riya said, her voice steady though her grip on her sword tightened. "We've faced your trials. We'll face you too."

Raktashak's smile widened, his glowing eyes narrowing with disdain. "Brave words, warrior. But bravery will not save you. The Sankalp Shila will be mine, and with it, I will reshape Aryavrata. You cannot stop what is coming."

Bharat's pulse raced. He knew Raktashak was powerful, but standing here, facing the sorcerer's dark presence, he felt the full weight of just how dangerous their enemy truly was. The air around him felt heavy, suffocating. He could feel Raktashak's eyes on him, piercing through his very soul.

"I've heard of you," Raktashak said, his eyes locking onto Bharat. "The outsider. The one from the prophecy." His voice was filled with mockery. "You think you can stop me? You, who does not even belong to this world?"

Bharat swallowed hard, his throat dry. His mind raced, the fear gnawing at him, but he couldn't back down. Not now. Not after everything they had been through. "I may not know what I'm capable of yet," Bharat said, his voice shaking slightly but growing steadier with each word. "But I know I won't let you destroy this world."

Raktashak's laughter echoed through the ravine, cold and cruel. "Such arrogance. You will fail, outsider. You will fail, just like all the others."

And with that, Raktashak raised his hand, and the darkness surged toward them, a wave of dark energy that pulsed with malevolent power. Bharat barely had time to react before the force of it hit them, knocking the breath from his lungs and sending him sprawling to the ground.

Riya was on her feet in an instant, her sword flashing as she deflected the next wave of dark energy. The blade glowed with a fierce, otherworldly light as it clashed with Raktashak's magic.

"Stay close!" she shouted, her voice tense. "We need to work together if we're going to beat him!"

Aarav scrambled to his feet, pulling a small vial from his satchel. The liquid inside glowed with a soft blue light. "This is a purification elixir," he explained quickly. "It should weaken his magic, but we have to get close enough to use it."

Bharat nodded, his mind racing as he tried to come up with a plan. "Riya, can you distract him? Aarav and I will try to get close enough to use the elixir."

Riya gave a curt nod, her eyes blazing with determination. "I'll keep him busy. Just be quick."

With a fierce battle cry, Riya charged at Raktashak, her sword swinging in wide arcs as she struck at the sorcerer with all her strength. Raktashak's eyes gleamed with amusement as he deflected each blow effortlessly, his dark magic swirling around him like a protective barrier.

"You think you can defeat me with that toy?" Raktashak sneered, his voice dripping with disdain. "You are nothing but a fool."

But Riya was relentless. Each strike was more forceful than the last as she pushed Raktashak back, creating an opening for Bharat and Aarav to move in.

"Now!" Aarav whispered urgently, and the two of them darted forward, keeping low to the ground as they made their way toward Raktashak.

The darkness around the sorcerer pulsed and writhed, the shadows growing thicker with each passing moment. Bharat could feel the weight of it pressing down on him, a suffocating force that threatened to overwhelm him. His heart raced in his chest as they neared Raktashak, the elixir clutched tightly in Aarav's hand.

But just as they were about to strike, Raktashak turned, his glowing eyes narrowing as he spotted them.

"You dare!" he roared, his voice filled with fury.

With a flick of his wrist, he unleashed a powerful wave of dark magic, sending Bharat and Aarav flying backward. The force of the blast knocked the vial from Aarav's hand, and it skittered across the ground, the glowing liquid spilling out onto the rocks.

"No!" Aarav cried, scrambling to retrieve the vial, but Raktashak was faster. With a cruel smile, he crushed the vial beneath his heel, the remaining liquid seeping into the ground and disappearing into the darkness.

"Did you really think you could defeat me with such pitiful tricks?" Raktashak sneered, his voice filled with contempt.

Bharat struggled to his feet, his body aching from the impact. "We're not done yet," he said, his voice defiant despite the fear that gnawed at him.

Raktashak's eyes gleamed with malice as he raised his hand once more. "You will be."

Before Bharat could react, Raktashak unleashed another blast of dark energy, the force of it slamming into Bharat like a tidal wave. The darkness closed in around him, suffocating him, crushing him under its weight. His vision blurred, and for a moment, he thought he might lose consciousness.

But even as the darkness threatened to overwhelm him, a spark of light flickered within him. A spark of hope, of determination. Bharat clenched his fists, drawing on every ounce of strength he had left. He couldn't give up. Not now. Not when everything was at stake.

With a surge of willpower, Bharat forced himself to stand, the light within him growing brighter, pushing back against the darkness.

"You will not defeat me," Bharat whispered, his voice barely audible but filled with resolve. "I won't let you."

The light within him flared, breaking through the darkness like a beacon. The shadows recoiled, the darkness retreating as Bharat took a step forward.

Raktashak's eyes widened in surprise, a flicker of uncertainty crossing his face. "Impossible," he muttered, his voice filled with disbelief.

Bharat stood tall, his resolve unshakable. “This isn’t over, Raktashak. We will stop you.”

With a snarl of rage, Raktashak unleashed one final blast of dark magic, the ground beneath them shaking from the force of it. But this time, Bharat was ready. His light shielded him, pushing back against the darkness.

Riya and Aarav rushed to his side, their determination matching his own. Together, they stood against Raktashak, their combined strength forcing the darkness back.

For a moment, it seemed as though they might succeed. The darkness around Raktashak flickered, the shadows wavering as the light from Bharat, Riya, and Aarav pushed it back.

But Raktashak was far from defeated. With a roar of fury, he drew upon the full extent of his power, the darkness swelling and crashing over them like a tidal wave.

The last thing Bharat heard was Raktashak’s cold laughter, echoing through the darkness as everything went black.

When Bharat awoke, the world around him had changed. The ravine was gone, replaced by a barren, desolate landscape. The sky was a sickly grey, and the air was heavy with the stench of decay.

Riya and Aarav were beside him, their expressions filled with concern and confusion.

“Where are we?” Bharat asked, his voice hoarse.

“This... this isn’t Aryavrata anymore,” Aarav said, his voice trembling. “Raktashak’s magic... it’s warped this place. We’re in his domain now. The Shadow Realm.”

A cold chill ran down Bharat’s spine. They had been pulled into Raktashak’s world, a place where darkness reigned supreme. The stakes had never been higher.

But despite the fear that gnawed at him, Bharat knew they couldn't give up. They had come too far. The Sankalp Shila was within reach, and they had to stop Raktashak.

With renewed determination, Bharat pushed himself to his feet, his gaze fixed on the horizon. "We'll find a way out of this. And when we do, we'll finish what we started."

Riya and Aarav nodded, their resolve matching his own. Together, they would face the darkness, confront Raktashak, and claim the Sankalp Shila.

The final battle was drawing near, and with it, the fate of Aryavrata would be decided.

CHAPTER IX

The Shadow Realm

The oppressive silence of the barren land was overwhelming. The once lush and vibrant landscape of Aryavrata had transformed into a cold, grey wasteland, as if all life had been drained from it. The sky hung heavy and dark, casting a dim, sickly light over the cracked, lifeless ground. It was a place where hope seemed to wither and die—a place shaped by Raktashak's malevolent magic.

Bharat, Riya, and Aarav stood on the edge of this desolation, their expressions filled with a mixture of dread and determination. They had been pulled into Raktashak's twisted domain—the Shadow Realm—and now the path ahead was more uncertain than ever. Bharat shivered as the cold bit into his skin, but it wasn't just the temperature. It was the oppressive weight of the atmosphere that pressed down on him. Every breath felt thick, heavy with despair, like the land itself was suffocating him.

"This is what Raktashak's darkness does," Riya said quietly, her voice edged with anger. Her piercing green eyes, usually so focused, now darted around warily. She tightened her grip on the hilt of her sword. "It corrupts, destroys, until there's nothing left but emptiness."

Aarav, ever the logical one, gazed out at the desolate land, his brow furrowed in concentration. "This isn't just any barren place. We're trapped in a realm where reality itself bends to Raktashak's will. The very laws of nature are warped here. We need to be cautious—there's no telling what dangers could be lurking."

Bharat took a deep breath, trying to steady himself. The air tasted foul, as if tainted by decay. Each step forward felt like pushing against an invisible force that wanted them to stop. He glanced at his companions, the battle-hardened Riya with her armour scuffed but still gleaming, and the ever-focused Aarav with his satchel of scrolls and magical tools. They looked just as worn as he felt. But there was no turning back now.

"We have to keep moving," Bharat said, his voice firm, though he was speaking more to himself than to the others. His heart raced, but he couldn't show weakness. Not here, not now. "Raktashak is trying to break us, but we can't give in. We need to find a way out of this cursed realm."

Riya's eyes narrowed, and she nodded sharply. "He won't win. We've faced worse, and we'll face him too. Let's just stay alert. This is more than a wasteland—he's watching us, manipulating the land. Don't let your guard down."

Bharat clenched his fists, trying to ignore the gnawing sense of dread that crawled up his spine. The land around them felt alive in the worst possible way—like it was waiting for them to make a mistake. The ground was uneven, filled with jagged rocks and twisted, dead trees. The sky was a dull grey, oppressive and thick, and the air clung to them like a suffocating blanket.

As they walked, Bharat noticed something strange. The landscape seemed to ripple, almost like a mirage. First a tree appeared too close, then too far. The horizon twisted in ways that defied logic, and he began to feel dizzy as if the land itself was playing tricks on them.

"Is it just me, or does it feel like we're not getting anywhere?" Bharat asked, his voice laced with frustration. "It's like we're walking in circles."

Aarav looked around, his brows drawn together in thought. "No, it's not you. Raktashak's magic is distorting the landscape. He's trying to trap us in this nightmare, making us lose hope."

Riya's jaw tightened as she scanned their surroundings. "He's toying with us. But we're not going to let him win. We'll find a way through this."

Suddenly, the ground beneath them began to tremble, and a low, ominous rumble filled the air. Bharat's heart jumped in his chest as cracks began to form in the earth. From those cracks, dark, writhing shapes began to emerge, slithering up from the ground like serpents made of pure shadow.

"Get back!" Riya shouted, her voice sharp and commanding.

The three of them leaped away as the dark shadows—more like creeping vines or slithering ropes of darkness—reached out, striking the ground where they had just stood. These shadowy ropes twisted and curled, reaching for them with unnatural speed, like dark tendrils hunting prey.

Bharat's pulse quickened. The sight of those shadowy shapes sent a chill down his spine. They moved like living creatures, but there was no life in them—just pure, malevolent darkness.

"Raktashak's trying to drag us deeper into the shadows," Aarav said, his voice tight with alarm. "We can't let them touch us!"

Bharat's heart pounded as he dodged the creeping ropes of shadow. Each swipe felt too close, as if the darkness itself was trying to consume him. He could feel the malevolence radiating from the dark shapes—they weren't just trying to ensnare them; they wanted to swallow them whole, drag them into the depths of the Shadow Realm.

"This is insane!" Bharat gasped, his breath coming in short bursts. "We can't just keep running and fighting them off—they're not going to stop!"

Riya's eyes darted toward a jagged rock formation up ahead. "There!" she called, pointing. "We can use those rocks for cover!"

They sprinted towards the rocks, the shadowy ropes twisting and lunging at them, almost as if they were alive and hunting. Bharat's legs burned from the effort, but the fear driving him was stronger than the pain. The cold, unnatural air bit at his skin, and the shadows felt like they were closing in.

As they reached the safety of the rocks, Riya swung her sword in a wide arc, slicing through one of the shadowy ropes. The darkness recoiled with a screeching hiss, but more shadows surged forward, seemingly endless in their pursuit.

"This isn't working," Bharat panted, his chest heaving. His arms felt like lead, and his mind was racing. "We can't just keep running and fighting them off—they're not going to stop!"

Aarav's gaze flickered around, his mind working furiously. "We need to sever Raktashak's control over this place. He's using the land itself to keep us trapped. If we can weaken his hold, we can escape."

"But how do we break his hold?" Bharat asked, trying to think through the rising panic. Every fibre of his being was screaming to keep moving, to avoid the shadowy ropes that kept lunging at them.

Aarav's eyes focused on something in the distance—a dark figure hovering at the far edge of the barren land. It was Raktashak, a shadowy figure who loomed over the landscape, his presence suffocating. His very existence seemed to radiate darkness, and Bharat felt his stomach churn just looking at him.

"There!" Aarav pointed. "That's where his control is strongest. He's connected to this realm. If we sever that connection, we can break free."

Riya didn't hesitate. "Let's go. We'll fight our way through." Her determination was unshaken, her hand steady on her sword.

They charged toward Raktashak, sprinting across the jagged terrain as the shadowy ropes continued to chase them. Bharat's legs burned with each step, but he forced himself to keep going, driven by the fear of being swallowed by the darkness. The ropes lashed out, but they managed to dodge, duck, and weave through the assault, barely avoiding the shadows' grasp.

As they neared Raktashak, the air grew even colder, and the ground beneath them seemed to pulse with dark energy. Bharat could feel it—Raktashak's presence was suffocating, a black hole of malevolence. His stomach twisted in fear, but he couldn't stop now.

Raktashak turned slowly to face them, his eyes glowing with malice. His twisted smile sent chills down Bharat's spine, and his voice dripped with contempt.

"You think you can defy me?" Raktashak's voice was a low, guttural growl, echoing through the barren land. "This place is my domain. The darkness bends to my will."

Bharat swallowed hard, his throat dry with fear, but he forced himself to meet Raktashak's gaze. "We're not staying here. We're getting out."

Raktashak's laughter was cold and cruel. "Escape? There is no escape. You are trapped in my world. This place will devour you, and there will be nothing left."

Riya stepped forward, her sword gleaming in the dim light. “We’ve beaten your tricks before, Raktashak. We’ll do it again.”

Raktashak’s eyes narrowed, and with a flick of his wrist, he sent a wave of darkness rushing toward them. The force of the dark magic slammed into them, nearly knocking them off their feet. Bharat stumbled, gasping as the shadows clawed at him, suffocating him with their cold, oppressive weight.

Just as he was trying to regain his balance, Raktashak unleashed another blast of dark energy, this time aimed directly at Bharat. The blow struck him full force in the chest, sending him flying across the rocky ground. He hit the earth hard, the impact knocking the wind out of him, his vision spinning as his head collided with a sharp rock.

Pain exploded through Bharat’s body, his mind reeling from the impact. For a moment, he couldn’t think, couldn’t breathe. His vision blurred as the edges of his consciousness darkened. Everything felt distant, surreal, as if he were watching the scene unfold from far away.

Through the haze of pain, Bharat saw Riya and Aarav still fighting. Riya swung her sword fiercely, but Raktashak’s power was overwhelming. Aarav was chanting, trying to summon a spell, but he was barely holding his own. Bharat’s chest tightened with fear as he saw Raktashak turn toward his friends.

“No,” Bharat whispered, his voice barely audible. He tried to push himself up, but his limbs felt heavy, uncooperative. His body screamed in protest, every movement sending sharp jolts of pain through him.

Raktashak unleashed another blast of dark magic, and Bharat watched in horror as his friends were thrown to the ground, their weapons scattering from their hands. Riya struggled to get up, her face etched with pain, while Aarav lay motionless for a moment before weakly stirring.

Bharat's heart pounded in his chest, his mind racing. He couldn't let this happen. Not here. Not like this.

He closed his eyes, his breath coming in ragged gasps as he reached deep within himself. He could feel the light still flickering inside him, faint but present. It was warm, steady, like a beacon in the darkness. But it was so hard to focus—Raktashak's magic was crushing, suffocating, drowning out everything else.

"You are nothing," Raktashak's voice echoed through the air. "You cannot defeat me."

Bharat gritted his teeth, forcing himself to push past the pain, past the fear. He had to focus. He had to find the light. He closed his eyes, shutting out the world around him, shutting out the sight of his friends lying on the ground. All that mattered was the light.

Slowly, agonisingly, Bharat felt the warmth within him begin to grow. The light expanded, filling him with a sense of calm, of strength. It was small at first, but with every breath, it grew brighter, stronger. He could feel it pushing back against the darkness, cutting through the suffocating weight of Raktashak's magic.

The ground beneath Raktashak began to tremble, cracks forming in the earth as Bharat's light grew stronger. Raktashak's eyes widened in fury, his voice filled with venom.

"You dare challenge me? You are NOTHING!"

But Bharat didn't falter. He focused all his energy, channelling every ounce of strength he had left into the light. The earth shook violently, and a blinding light erupted from the ground beneath Raktashak's feet. The shadowy ropes recoiled, shrinking back into the earth as the darkness was driven away.

"No!" Raktashak roared, his voice filled with rage and desperation. "You cannot escape me!"

But it was too late. Bharat's light had severed Raktashak's hold on the land. The Shadow Realm began to dissolve around them, the oppressive darkness lifting as the real world started to break through.

Bharat collapsed to the ground, gasping for air as the weight of the dark magic disappeared. His body ached with exhaustion, but a wave of relief washed over him. They had done it. They had broken free.

As the light cleared, Bharat blinked in astonishment at the sight before him. The barren wasteland had vanished, replaced by a breathtaking landscape of rolling green hills, sparkling streams, and the majestic final temple standing in the distance.

The temple's ancient stone walls were adorned with intricate carvings, glowing softly in the sunlight. The air was fresh, filled with the scent of wildflowers and the sound of birdsong. It was as if they had stepped into a different world entirely.

"We... we made it," Bharat whispered, his voice thick with awe and relief.

Riya pushed herself to her feet, her face a mixture of exhaustion and determination. "We're not trapped anymore. We've broken free."

Aarav, still breathing heavily, wiped the sweat from his brow. "We've weakened him. He can't control us here."

Bharat's body screamed with exhaustion, but his resolve remained unshaken. "But it's not over yet."

Aarav nodded. "We need to find the Sankalp Shila before Raktashak regains his strength."

Riya sheathed her sword, her fierce spirit undiminished by the trials they had faced. “Let’s finish this.”

And so, with their hearts steeled and their resolve unbroken, Bharat, Riya, and Aarav pressed on, ready for the final battle. The fate of Aryavrata rested on their shoulders, and they would do whatever it took to protect it.

CHAPTER X

Sankalp Shila

The sun had broken through the oppressive clouds that had hung over them during their escape from the Shadow Realm, casting a soft, warm light on the landscape. The air was clear, fresh, and fragrant with the scent of wildflowers and lush greenery. Bharat, Riya, and Aarav stood still for a moment, basking in the sudden change, taking in the serenity of the scene before them. The warmth of the sun on Bharat's skin was a welcome relief after the icy cold of the Shadow Realm. He closed his eyes, allowing himself a brief moment of peace.

"We did it," Riya whispered, her voice filled with awe and disbelief. She sheathed her sword, her face softened by the gentle warmth of the sun. "We're really out."

Aarav exhaled, letting out a breath he had been holding. "I wasn't sure we'd make it," he admitted, his usually calm expression giving way to a rare smile. "It feels like a dream."

Bharat took a deep breath, letting the fresh air fill his lungs. The oppressive weight of the Shadow Realm had lifted, and for the first time in what felt like ages, he felt truly alive. He shared a glance with Riya and Aarav, a small smile tugging at the corners of his mouth.

"It's not over yet," Bharat said, his voice calm, though there was an unmistakable note of relief. "But we're close."

The three of them stood on a small hill, gazing out over a verdant valley. Rolling hills of green stretched out before them, dotted with wildflowers in shades of purple, yellow, and white. A stream sparkled in the distance, its water clear and pure as it meandered through the landscape. Birds chirped in the trees, their songs filling the air with a sense of normalcy that had been absent for so long.

At the far end of the valley stood the final temple. It was majestic, carved from stone that gleamed in the sunlight, its ancient walls covered in intricate carvings and glowing symbols. The structure was vast, with towering spires that reached toward the sky, and a massive archway that seemed to beckon them inside. The temple radiated power, its very presence commanding respect.

"This must be it," Aarav said quietly, his eyes fixed on the temple. "The Temple of Kshatra. The last place we need to go."

Riya nodded, her eyes narrowing as she focused on the distant structure. "That's where the Sankalp Shila is. The final battle is ahead."

But for now, they allowed themselves to revel in the momentary peace. The weather was warm, the breeze gentle, and the tension of their journey seemed to melt away in the sunlight. Bharat could almost forget the danger that still loomed ahead.

Then, without warning, the sky darkened.

The warmth of the sun vanished, replaced by an icy chill that sent shivers down Bharat's spine. The birds stopped singing, and the once gentle breeze turned into a biting wind that whipped through the valley. The green hills, once bathed in golden light, were now cast in shadow.

Bharat's heart sank as a sense of dread washed over him. He knew what this meant. He could feel it in the air—Raktashak was close.

Riya's hand instinctively went to the hilt of her sword, her posture tense and alert. "He's here," she muttered, her voice low and filled with anger. "Raktashak is inside the temple."

Aarav nodded grimly, his face pale. "He's trying to stop us. He knows we're close."

Bharat's stomach twisted with a mix of fear and determination. The peace they had felt just moments ago was gone, replaced by the suffocating presence of Raktashak's dark magic. The weight of the task ahead settled heavily on his shoulders, but there was no turning back now.

"We have to face him," Bharat said, his voice steady despite the fear gnawing at him. "This is our only chance."

Riya and Aarav exchanged glances, both of them nodding in agreement. There was no need for more words—they all knew what was at stake.

Together, they descended the hill and made their way toward the temple, the dark clouds above swirling ominously as if the sky itself was conspiring against them. The wind howled around them, carrying with it the faint echoes of a malevolent laughter that chilled Bharat to the bone. Every step they took felt heavier, as if the land itself was resisting their approach.

When they finally reached the entrance of the temple, the oppressive weight of Raktashak's presence was nearly suffocating. The ancient stone walls of the Temple of Kshatra loomed before them, etched with glowing symbols that pulsed with an eerie inner light. The carvings depicted scenes of battles long past, warriors locked in combat, and mystical forces swirling around them. The air inside the temple hummed with a palpable energy, as if the very stones themselves were alive with power.

Bharat stared up at the massive archway that led inside, his heart pounding in his chest. This was it—the final challenge. Inside, the Sankalp Shila awaited, and so did Raktashak.

"This is it," Riya said quietly, her voice filled with determination. "The Sankalp Shila is inside. But so is Raktashak."

Aarav stepped forward, his expression grim as he studied the carvings on the walls. "We've weakened him, but he's not defeated. We need to be prepared for anything. Once we enter, there's no turning back."

Bharat felt a heavy weight settle in his chest as he looked at his companions. They had come so far, faced so many challenges, and now they were on the brink of the final battle. But something still gnawed at him, a lingering doubt that he couldn't shake.

As they approached the entrance, Aarav suddenly stopped and turned to Bharat. His face was serious, a mixture of concern and resolve in his eyes.

"Bharat, before we go any further, there's something I need to tell you," Aarav began, his voice low and measured.

Bharat looked at him, sensing the weight of the moment. "What is it, Aarav?"

Aarav took a deep breath, as if steeling himself for what he was about to say. "The Sankalp Shila is not just a powerful artifact. It's bound by ancient laws—laws that demand a price for its use. The Shila's power can only be fully unlocked by someone who is willing to make a significant sacrifice. That sacrifice is different for everyone, but it's always something deeply personal, something that defines you."

Bharat felt a cold shiver run down his spine. The thought of losing something precious was daunting, but at the same time, he knew that the fate of Aryavrata was at stake. If he didn't do whatever it took to stop Raktashak, this world—and everyone in it—would be lost.

"What do you mean by 'sacrifice'? What would I have to give up?"

Aarav hesitated for a moment, then continued, his voice filled with a mix of regret and urgency. "The Shila tests you, Bharat. It knows what you value most, and it will demand that you give it up in order to save Aryavrata. The nature of the sacrifice is something you won't fully understand until the moment comes, but it will be something you hold dear."

The weight of Aarav's words settled heavily on Bharat's shoulders, and he felt a wave of fear and uncertainty wash over him. His mind raced as he tried to comprehend the gravity of what Aarav was saying. Sacrifice something that defined him? It sounded too abstract, yet ominous at the same time.

Riya stepped closer, placing a reassuring hand on Bharat's shoulder. Her voice was gentle but firm. "Bharat, whatever happens, we're with you. We'll face this together."

Bharat looked at Riya, her fierce determination and unwavering loyalty shining in her eyes. He then turned to Aarav, who gave him a nod of encouragement. They had been through so much together, and now they were on the brink of the final battle. Whatever the Shila demanded of him, Bharat knew he couldn't let his friends—or Aryavrata—down.

Taking a deep breath, Bharat squared his shoulders and nodded. "I understand. Whatever the Shila demands, I'll face it. Let's end this."

With renewed determination, the trio stepped into the temple, the air around them humming with an almost palpable energy. The interior of the temple was vast, its walls lined with ancient carvings that seemed to come alive with the flickering light of the torches. The floor was covered in intricate patterns, and the air was filled with the faint scent of incense and something more ancient—something powerful.

As they walked deeper into the temple, the atmosphere grew heavier, as if the very air was charged with anticipation. The path led them to a large, circular chamber at the heart of the temple, where the Sankalp Shila rested on a raised pedestal. The crystal was larger than Bharat had imagined, its surface smooth and gleaming with a soft, inner light that seemed to pulse in time with the beating of a heart.

"There it is," Riya whispered, her voice filled with awe. "The Sankalp Shila."

Aarav approached the Shila cautiously, his eyes wide with reverence. "This is the source of all the legends, all the power... It's even more magnificent than I ever imagined."

Bharat felt a strange pull towards the Shila, as if it were calling to him, drawing him closer. He stepped forward, his heart pounding in his chest as he reached out to touch the crystal. The moment his fingers brushed the surface, a surge of energy shot through him, and the chamber around them began to tremble.

"Bharat, wait!" Aarav called out, his voice filled with urgency. "Before you activate the Shila, you need to understand what you're about to do."

Bharat hesitated, his hand hovering over the crystal. "What do you mean?"

Aarav took a deep breath, his expression serious. "Once you activate the Shila, there's no turning back. It will test you, demand your sacrifice, and if you're found worthy, it will grant you the power to defeat Raktashak. But if you hesitate, if you're not willing to give up what it demands, it could destroy you."

Bharat swallowed hard, the weight of Aarav's words pressing down on him. This was it—the moment of truth. The fate of Aryavrata, and possibly his own, hinged on what he was about to do. He glanced at Riya, who gave him a nod of encouragement, and then back at Aarav.

"I understand," Bharat said quietly, his voice steady despite the fear gnawing at him. "I'm ready."

As Bharat placed his hand on the Sankalp Shila, a blinding light filled the chamber, and he felt himself being pulled into a vortex of energy. The world around him dissolved, and he found himself standing in a vast, empty void, surrounded by nothing but an endless expanse of white light.

For a moment, Bharat felt completely alone, adrift in the void. But then, a voice echoed through the emptiness—a voice that was neither male nor female, neither young nor old. It was a voice that seemed to come from everywhere and nowhere at once, filled with an ancient wisdom that transcended time.

"You have come seeking the power of the Sankalp Shila," the voice said, its tone calm and measured. "But power comes with a price. What are you willing to sacrifice to save Aryavrata?"

Bharat's heart pounded in his chest as he realised that this was the test—the moment when he would have to face the Shila's demands. "I'm willing to give whatever it takes," he replied, his voice trembling slightly. "But I don't know what that sacrifice is yet."

The voice seemed to consider his words for a moment, and then it spoke again. "The Shila knows what you value most, what you hold dear. It will demand that you give it up in exchange for its power. Are you prepared to make that sacrifice?"

Bharat took a deep breath, his mind racing. He thought of his life on Earth, of the family and friends he had left behind. But these thoughts were only fleeting, as the voice seemed to probe deeper, reaching into the very core of his being.

He felt a strange tug at his heart, a sensation that he couldn't quite place. It wasn't fear, but a profound realisation that the Shila was asking for something that would change him forever. His thoughts grew cloudy, and images flashed before him—memories, desires, his very sense of self.

"I am," Bharat said finally, his voice filled with resolve. "If it means saving this world, I'm prepared to give whatever it takes."

The voice was silent for a moment, and then it spoke again, its tone tinged with approval. "You have chosen wisely. The power of the Sankalp Shila is now yours."

As the words echoed through the void, Bharat felt a surge of energy course through him, filling him with a warmth and light that seemed to radiate from his very soul. The void around him began to dissolve, and he found himself back in the chamber, the light of the Shila pulsing in time with his heartbeat.

Riya and Aarav rushed to his side, their expressions filled with concern. "Bharat, are you okay?" Riya asked, her voice laced with worry.

Bharat nodded slowly, his mind still reeling from the experience. "I'm fine," he said quietly. "The Shila... it...accepted my sacrifice."

Aarav's eyes widened in realisation. "You... you gave up something important, didn't you?"

Bharat nodded, the weight of his decision settling over him like a heavy shroud. "I didn't understand at first, but now I do. The Shila demanded something that I hold dear, something that defines me. I gave that up to save Aryavrata."

Riya's eyes softened with sympathy, her hand tightening on his shoulder. "We're with you, Bharat. You made the right choice."

Bharat took a deep breath, trying to steady himself. The realisation of what he had given up was still sinking in, but there was no time to dwell on it now. The final battle was at hand, and Raktashak was still out there, waiting for them.

"Let's go," Bharat said, his voice filled with quiet determination. "We need to finish this."

With the power of the Sankalp Shila now coursing through him, Bharat felt a renewed sense of purpose. Whatever the cost, he was ready to face Raktashak and protect Aryavrata from the darkness that threatened to consume it.

Together, they turned towards the exit of the chamber, ready to face whatever challenges lay ahead. The fate of Aryavrata rested on their shoulders, and they would do whatever it took to protect it.

CHAPTER XI

Shadows of the Past

The Sankalp Shila rested in Bharat's hands, its warmth steady but heavy, like the weight of a destiny he hadn't fully understood when he first entered Aryavrata. Its soft glow pulsed with each beat of his heart, a constant reminder of the sacrifice he had accepted but couldn't fully comprehend. As they walked through the narrow stone passageways of the ancient temple, the air around them buzzed with tension, and every step echoed against the ancient walls like a countdown to something inevitable.

The further they ventured into the temple, the more Bharat's thoughts drifted away from the present, and into the past—back to Earth, back to the people he had left behind. He could still feel the presence of the Sankalp Shila entwined with his soul, and with each step, his memories seemed to blur and fade, as though the Shila was draining them away.

He remembered his father. It was a memory from when he was younger, perhaps ten or eleven. They had been sitting together in the living room, his father reading the newspaper while Bharat fidgeted with his school books. His father, ever the quiet man, had put down the paper and started telling him about his travels—adventures to distant places for work, places Bharat had always dreamed of visiting.

"Someday, Bharat, you'll see the world too," his father had said, his eyes twinkling with quiet pride. "It's big and full of surprises, but you've got to be brave. You've got to take that first step."

Bharat's heart ached at the memory, but something was wrong. His father's voice—usually so clear, so strong—felt distant, as if being whispered through a fog. And his face... Bharat tried to picture his father's face, but it was fading. The more he focused on it, the blurrier it became, until he could barely remember the colour of his eyes or the lines of his smile.

It was as though the more he clung to the past, the more the memories slipped away.

Next, he remembered his mother. He could see her now, standing in their kitchen, her hands deftly preparing a meal as the soft clinking of pots and pans filled the air. She had always hummed as she cooked, a soft melody that she had learned from her mother. Bharat used to sit on the counter, watching her, comforted by the warmth of home.

"Bharat, beta, finish your homework before dinner," she would say, glancing at him with that soft, maternal smile that could ease any worry.

But now, as Bharat tried to recall that memory, the details were slipping. He couldn't remember if she had worn a sari or a salwar kameez that day. He couldn't remember the exact tone of her voice, the words she had spoken. It was as though the memory was unravelling right before his eyes, piece by piece, fading into oblivion.

"Ma..." he whispered, his voice barely audible.

Riya, walking beside him, glanced over, sensing his turmoil but choosing to remain silent. She could see the storm in his eyes—the quiet struggle he was trying so hard to hide.

And then there was Meera. Her memory was the hardest to bear. Meera had been his anchor back on Earth, his confidante, the one person who had known him better than anyone else. He could still see her in his mind, her dark hair flowing in the sea breeze as they sat by the shore at Marine Drive. They had spent so many evenings there, watching the waves crash against the rocks, talking about everything and nothing.

"I want to travel the world with you, Bharat," she had said one night, her voice soft but full of excitement. "There's so much to see, so much to experience. Let's make a life full of stories."

But now, that memory—once so vivid and real—was beginning to blur too. Bharat could no longer hear her laughter as clearly as before, and when he tried to picture her face, it was like looking through a foggy window. His heart twisted painfully. Was that the price he had paid? Was it the memories of the people he loved most?

The thought hit him like a punch to the gut. He had agreed to give up something precious in exchange for the power of the Sankalp Shila. But he hadn't expected it to be this. He hadn't expected it to feel like losing pieces of himself.

"Bharat?" Aarav's voice broke through his thoughts, pulling him back to the present.

Bharat blinked, shaking off the haze of memories. He turned to see Aarav and Riya watching him, their faces etched with concern. They were walking through the final stretch of the temple, the ancient stone walls surrounding them adorned with intricate carvings that glowed faintly in the dim light.

"Are you alright?" Riya asked, her hand resting on the hilt of her sword, her green eyes focused on Bharat with a sharpness that showed she was ready for anything.

"I'm fine," Bharat said, though the weight of his lie sat heavy on his chest. He wasn't fine. His memories—his life back on Earth—were slipping away, and he had no idea how to stop it.

But now wasn't the time to dwell on what was lost. They were close to the end of their journey, and the fate of Aryavrata was hanging in the balance. There would be time later to mourn what had been taken.

As they continued walking, the air around them began to shift. What had been a warm and almost serene atmosphere outside the temple was now growing cold. The stone walls seemed to vibrate with an eerie energy, and the symbols etched into them glowed more intensely, as if responding to an unseen force.

Aarav looked around, his brow furrowed. "Do you feel that? Something's changed."

Bharat nodded. He could feel it too—the oppressive weight that had settled over them, thickening the air like a storm about to break. The warmth that had filled the temple earlier was gone, replaced by a bone-chilling cold that gnawed at his skin.

"He's here," Riya whispered, her grip tightening on her sword.

They reached the end of the narrow corridor, the heavy stone doors before them creaking open as if sensing their arrival. Beyond the doors lay the exit to the temple—a long stone staircase that led down into the open air. But as they stepped through, the cold hit them like a wave, and a dark shadow loomed over the landscape.

Bharat's heart raced as he looked up.

There, at the base of the stairs, stood Raktashak.

The air seemed to crackle with dark energy as Raktashak's twisted form emerged from the shadows. His eyes glowed with a malevolent light, and the darkness surrounding him pulsed with an eerie rhythm. The very ground seemed to tremble under his presence, as if the land itself recoiled from his power.

"You've come far, little ones," Raktashak said, his voice a low, guttural growl that sent chills down Bharat's spine. "But this is where your journey ends."

Bharat clenched his fists, the Sankalp Shila glowing brightly in his hands. He could feel its power coursing through him, but the weight of it pressed down on his soul, a constant reminder of the price he had paid.

"We're not afraid of you, Raktashak," Riya said, stepping forward, her sword gleaming in the fading light. "We've beaten your traps, and we'll beat you too."

Raktashak's lips curled into a cruel smile. "Brave words, warrior. But bravery alone won't save you."

Aarav moved beside Bharat, his eyes focused on Raktashak. "We have the Sankalp Shila now," he said, his voice steady but filled with determination. "Your time is over."

Raktashak's laughter echoed through the air, cold and mocking. "You think the Shila will save you? You've only scratched the surface of its power. You don't even understand the price you've paid."

Bharat's chest tightened at the words. Raktashak's gaze seemed to bore into him, as if he knew the doubts swirling in Bharat's mind.

"I can feel it," Raktashak hissed. "The emptiness inside you. The loss. Do you even know what the Shila has taken from you?"

Bharat's heart pounded in his chest, his thoughts flashing back to the memories of his father, his mother, and Meera. The haze, the fading details, the loss of something he had held so dear but couldn't quite grasp anymore.

Raktashak's eyes gleamed with malice. "You gave up more than you know, Bharat. And in the end, it won't be enough."

Bharat swallowed hard, his grip tightening on the Shila. He didn't know what he had lost—not fully. But he knew one thing for certain: he couldn't let Raktashak win.

With a determined look, he stepped forward, the Sankalp Shila glowing brightly in his hands.

"We'll see about that," Bharat said, his voice steady and filled with resolve.

Raktashak's smile faded, replaced by a look of cold fury. The dark energy around him intensified, swirling like a storm ready to strike.

The final battle was about to begin.

CHAPTER XII

The Saviour of Realms

Raktashak loomed before them, his form wreathed in shadows that twisted and writhed like serpents. His eyes glowed with a sinister light, and his voice, when it came, was like the rumble of distant thunder. The oppressive atmosphere of the Shadow Realm still clung to the air around them, even though they had exited its grip. The once vibrant glow of the Sankalp Shila felt like the only barrier between them and absolute darkness. Bharat felt as though the air itself was thick, as if every breath he took required effort.

The landscape, so recently bathed in the warmth of Aryavarta, now seemed to suffocate beneath the weight of Raktashak's malevolent presence. The temple walls, towering over them, seemed to hum with the tension of the moment, their ancient carvings dimmed by the suffocating darkness that seemed to emanate from the sorcerer's very being.

"You've come to your end," Raktashak sneered, his voice a venomous hiss as his glowing eyes fixed on the Sankalp Shila in Bharat's hand. His gaze flickered with a greedy hunger, the kind of dark desire that only grows when one believes ultimate power is within reach. "You think you can wield that power against me? You are nothing but insects to be crushed beneath my heel!"

Bharat felt the weight of the Shila in his hand, its energy pulsing in time with his heartbeat. Each pulse sent a shiver through him, reminding him of the immense power he held. But that power was not without cost. The Shila demanded a sacrifice—a sacrifice Bharat had agreed to, but one he had yet to fully understand. He could feel something slipping away, a piece of himself that was slowly eroding, like the tide pulling grains of sand from the shore. Faces flickered through his mind: his father's stern but kind smile, his mother's gentle touch, Meera's laugh that had once made his heart race. But those faces, those memories, felt blurred now, like trying to remember a dream upon waking.

His chest tightened with the fear of what he had lost, but there was no turning back now. The fate of Aryavarta rested in his hands, and with it, the Shila's immense power. Raktashak had to be stopped.

Beside him, Riya stepped forward, her sword gleaming under the oppressive dim light that struggled against the shadowy forces surrounding them. Her face was set, every line of her body taut with determination. "We won't let you destroy Aryavarta, Raktashak," she said, her voice strong, though tinged with exhaustion. "We've come too far, fought too hard to let you win now."

Aarav, his hands glowing with arcane energy, stood on the other side, his gaze never leaving Raktashak's twisted form. His usually calm demeanour was marred by the strain of battle, yet his resolve remained unshaken. "The Sankalp Shila was never meant for destruction," Aarav said, his voice carrying a quiet, simmering fury. "It was meant to protect this world, and we will see that it fulfills its purpose."

Bharat stood between his two friends, the Sankalp Shila pulsing steadily in his hand. The weight of it pressed down on him, both physically and emotionally. He had been pulled into this world—Aryavarta—by forces beyond his comprehension. He had fought monsters, travelled through realms, and now stood at the final confrontation. And yet, a part of him still felt like that same journalist from Earth, out of place in a world of gods and sorcerers. The Shila's weight was more than just its physical presence—it was the burden of responsibility, of knowing that this power could save or doom an entire world. And what was worse, he had no idea what it had taken from him.

"You think you can challenge me?" Raktashak spat, his voice a deep growl that resonated through the very stones of the temple. "I am the darkness! You are nothing!"

With a wave of his hand, Raktashak unleashed a torrent of dark energy, the shadows around him coiling and twisting into massive tendrils of black magic that lashed out at them with a ferocity that took Bharat's breath away. The air hummed with dark magic, thickening with the scent of sulphur and decay. The force of the attack was like a storm, suffocating and relentless.

Riya moved with practised speed, her sword slicing through the air as she deflected the first wave of shadowy tendrils. "We've faced worse than you!" she shouted, her voice cutting through the chaos. But there was a strain in her tone, a weariness that spoke of the long road they had already travelled to reach this moment. Bharat could see the tremor in her arms as she swung, but she never faltered, never hesitated.

Aarav's fingers moved in intricate patterns as he summoned a shield of light, a protective barrier that flickered against the onslaught of darkness. "Hold the line!" he called, his voice tight with concentration. Even with his formidable powers, it was clear that Raktashak's magic was pushing them to their limits. The dark tendrils crashed against Aarav's shield like waves against a cliff, and with every impact, Bharat could see the strain etched into his friend's features.

But even as they fought back, Bharat could feel the tide of the battle turning against them. The weight of the Shila grew heavier in his hand, the light within it flickering like a candle in a storm. He knew what he had to do, but the cost still lingered in the back of his mind. What had he given up? What piece of himself had been taken in exchange for the power he now wielded?

"Bharat!" Aarav shouted, his voice strained as he struggled to maintain the shield against the onslaught. "Now! Use the Shila!"

Bharat looked down at the glowing crystal in his hand, its light growing more intense with each passing second. The power within it surged like a storm, desperate to be released. His heart pounded in his chest, and his hand trembled under the weight of the choice before him. The faces of his loved ones swam before his eyes—his mother, his father, Meera. But they were slipping away, like shadows in the fading light.

He closed his eyes, taking a deep breath as he focused on the one thing that mattered now: Aryavarta. The land he had come to love, the people who had become his friends, and the world that needed him now more than ever. Whatever he had lost, whatever the Shila had taken from him, he would face it later. Right now, there was only the fight before him.

"I will not let you destroy this world," Bharat said, his voice low but steady, filled with a quiet determination that surprised even him.

Raktashak's eyes narrowed, a flicker of uncertainty passing through them as the Shila's light intensified. The dark tendrils faltered for a moment, recoiling as if sensing the power about to be unleashed.

"You think you can defeat me?" Raktashak spat, his voice thick with venom. "I am eternal! You are nothing!"

With a wave of his hand, Raktashak unleashed a torrent of dark energy, the shadows surging forward like a tidal wave. Riya and Aarav sprang into action, their combined efforts forming a barrier of light that pushed back against the onslaught. But it was clear that they were struggling, the power of Raktashak's darkness threatening to overwhelm them.

"Bharat!" Aarav shouted, his voice strained. "Now! Use the Shila!"

Bharat, without hesitation, stepped forward, the Sankalp Shila glowing brighter in his hand. He could feel the power building within the crystal, a storm of energy that threatened to tear him apart if he didn't release it. With a deep breath, he focused on the vision of Aryavrata as it once was—a land of peace and prosperity, free from the corruption of darkness. He channelled that vision into the Shila, willing the stone to unleash its full power.

But nothing happened.

The light of the Shila flickered but dimmed, as if the crystal was resisting him. Bharat's heart raced. He could feel the immense power in his hand, but the stone would not respond.

"No!" Bharat gritted his teeth, panic creeping into his chest. "Why isn't it working?"

Raktashak's laughter grew louder, more sinister, as if he could sense Bharat's struggle. "You cannot wield it," he taunted. "You lack the will, the sacrifice."

Bharat's grip on the Shila tightened. His thoughts raced, but deep down, he knew Raktashak was right. The Shila demanded more than just power; it demanded sacrifice. Aarav had warned him that the stone required something deeply personal, something he valued most.

Without the sacrifice, the Shila would never work.

As the realisation hit him, Bharat felt a wave of dread wash over him. His sacrifice—what could it be? What could the Shila possibly demand of him that he wasn't already willing to give?

His mind raced back to the life he had left behind—his father, his mother, Meera. The people who had shaped him, loved him, made him who he was. Could that be it? Could the Shila be asking him to give up his life in Mumbai, his family, his career?

Bharat's breath caught in his throat as the truth settled over him like a heavy weight. Yes. That was the sacrifice. He would have to give up everything—his life as a journalist, the family he loved, the future he had always envisioned. The Sankalp Shila was demanding that he remain in Aryavrata forever, as its guardian.

He felt his heart break a little at the thought. Could he really do it? Could he give up his old life—his father's wisdom, his mother's warmth, and Meera's love? Memories of them flooded his mind: his father teaching him how to ride a bicycle as a child, his mother's comforting voice telling him bedtime stories, the way Meera would laugh at his terrible jokes. The images were vivid, painful in their beauty.

But Aryavrata needed him. Riya and Aarav needed him. The fate of this world rested in his hands, and if he didn't act, Raktashak would destroy everything.

Bharat closed his eyes, tears stinging at the edges, and focused on his memories. He saw his father's proud smile, his mother's gentle touch, and Meera's loving gaze. The life he had always wanted, the future he had envisioned—it was all there, just out of reach. But it wasn't his anymore. Not if he was going to save Aryavrata.

He felt the weight of the sacrifice settle over him like a heavy shroud. There was no turning back. He had to let go.

"I understand now," Bharat whispered to himself. His voice was thick with emotion, but his resolve had never been stronger. He raised the Sankalp Shila once more, this time with the full knowledge of what it demanded of him. "I accept the sacrifice."

As if in response, the Shila's light flared brightly, filling the entire chamber with a radiant glow. The warmth of the stone's energy surged through him, and Bharat felt a deep, powerful connection to the crystal. The Shila pulsed in time with his heartbeat, its energy no longer resisting him but flowing freely, as if the sacrifice had unlocked its true power.

Bharat could feel it—the full strength of the Sankalp Shila, an overwhelming force that filled him with both light and sorrow. He felt as though he were standing on the edge of two worlds—one foot still in his past life, and the other firmly rooted in Aryavrata.

But there was no going back.

The Shila responded to his will, its light growing brighter and brighter until it filled the entire chamber with a blinding radiance. The darkness recoiled, and Raktashak's eyes widened in horror as the light surged toward him, consuming the shadows that clung to his form.

"No! This cannot be!" Raktashak screamed, his voice filled with fury and desperation. His form began to dissolve, the darkness that had once given him strength now tearing him apart. "I am eternal! I am—"

But his words were cut off as the light of the Sankalp Shila overwhelmed him completely. Raktashak let out one final, anguished scream before his form shattered into countless fragments of shadow, which were swiftly obliterated by the Shila's radiance.

For a moment, there was only silence. The oppressive darkness that had filled the chamber was gone, replaced by a serene stillness. The light of the Shila dimmed slightly, its power now contained, as if it had fulfilled its purpose.

Riya and Aarav, both breathing heavily from the exertion of the battle, looked around in awe and relief.

"We did it," Riya said, her voice filled with a mixture of disbelief and joy. "We actually did it. Raktashak is gone!"

Aarav nodded, a triumphant smile spreading across his face. "The darkness has been defeated. Aryavrata is safe!"

Bharat felt a wave of relief wash over him as he watched Riya and Aarav's reactions. They had done it—they had saved Aryavrata from the clutches of darkness. But just as he was about to join them in their moment of triumph, he felt a strange sensation, as if the ground beneath him had suddenly vanished.

The world around him blurred, Riya and Aarav's voices fading into the distance. The chamber, the temple, everything seemed to dissolve into a bright, white light, leaving Bharat standing alone in a vast, empty space. The silence was absolute, and for a moment, Bharat wasn't sure if he was still alive or if he had somehow crossed into another realm.

For a moment, Bharat was completely alone. The emptiness around him was overwhelming, stretching endlessly in every direction. Time seemed to stop, and the weight of everything he had just done, everything he had lost, pressed down on him like a crushing wave. Was this the afterlife? Had he been defeated, or was this some kind of limbo?

But then, as his mind spun with confusion, a figure began to materialise before him—a being of light, not human but not entirely alien either. The figure was tall, its form shifting and changing as if made of pure energy. It seemed to glow with an inner radiance, a light that was soft yet powerful, comforting yet awe-inspiring. Its presence was overwhelming, yet it exuded a sense of calm and serenity, as if its mere existence was enough to soothe the chaos in Bharat's heart.

"Who are you?" Bharat asked, his voice trembling slightly as it echoed in the vast emptiness.

The figure's voice resonated in Bharat's mind, not spoken aloud but felt deep within his soul. It was a voice that transcended language, a communication that went straight to the core of his being. "I am a being beyond your understanding, one of the first to exist in this universe. I am neither alive nor dead, not bound by the laws that govern your world."

Bharat struggled to comprehend what he was hearing. His mind, already reeling from the battle and the sudden shift to this strange place, grasped at the words but found them almost too immense to fully understand. "Are you... are you a god?" he asked, his voice filled with uncertainty and awe.

The figure seemed to smile, though it had no discernible features. The light around it pulsed gently, as if amused by the question. "No, I am not a god. I am something more ancient, something that existed before the concept of gods came into being. I am a guide, a finder of those who are worthy to become guardians of the realms."

Bharat's mind raced with questions, each one more pressing than the last. The events of the past hours—days?—whirled through his thoughts. "What is this place? Why am I here?" he asked, his voice a mixture of fear and curiosity.

"This is a space between realms," the figure explained, its tone patient and measured, as if it had all the time in the world. "A place where the boundaries of reality are fluid, where those who have been chosen can converse with beings such as myself. You have been brought here because you have proven yourself worthy of the Sankalp Shila. It is not a mere artifact; it is a test, one that reveals those who are willing to sacrifice themselves for the greater good."

Bharat frowned, his thoughts catching on the word 'sacrifice.' He had felt the weight of the Shila's power, its demand for something more than just his courage. "So the stone doesn't demand a sacrifice?" he asked, his voice laced with uncertainty.

"No," the figure replied, its voice filled with a gentle certainty. "It only tests those who would be willing to make one. It seeks out those who are prepared to give everything for the sake of others. That is why it chose you, Bharat. You are now the guardian of Aryavrata."

Bharat felt a wave of disbelief wash over him. The enormity of what the figure was saying was almost too much to bear. "A guardian? But I'm just a journalist. I'm no hero," he protested, his voice cracking under the strain of the revelation.

"Every guardian starts as something ordinary," the figure said, its tone filled with a quiet wisdom that made Bharat feel like a child in the presence of a great teacher. "What makes them extraordinary is their willingness to protect their realm, to maintain the balance. Aryavrata is but one of many realms, each with its own guardian. Together, these guardians are known as the Saviours of

Realms."

Bharat was overwhelmed by the enormity of what he was hearing. His mind struggled to wrap around the idea that there were other realms, other guardians, each tasked with protecting a world as vast and complex as Aryavrata. "So, there are others like me?" he asked, his voice filled with both wonder and trepidation.

"Yes," the figure confirmed, its light pulsing softly in rhythm with its words. "Many others, each tasked with safeguarding their own realm. Some realms are filled with magic and wonder, like Aryavrata. Others are darker, more dangerous. But all are connected, and all must be protected."

Bharat nodded slowly, beginning to understand the gravity of his new role. The weight of it pressed down on him, but there was also a strange sense of peace that came with the knowledge. He wasn't alone in this—there were others out there, others who had faced the same trials, made the same sacrifices. "What happens now?" he asked, his voice quiet, almost reverent.

"You will return to your world," the figure said, its tone gentle yet firm. "But you will never be far from Aryavrata. The connection between you and your realm is eternal. While you may not always be able to find your way back physically, your spirit will always be intertwined with Aryavrata. In time, you may discover the way back."

Bharat felt a pang of sadness at the thought of leaving Aryavrata behind, even if only for a time. He had grown to love the land, the people, the very essence of the realm. And yet, there was a part of him that longed to return to Earth, to the life he had known. "But what if I want to go back? What if I want to return to Aryavrata?" he asked, his voice filled with a quiet desperation.

The figure's light began to intensify, growing brighter and brighter until it was almost blinding. "Remember, Bharat," the figure said, its voice echoing in Bharat's mind like a distant melody, "you are not alone. The Saviours of Realms are always with you, guiding and watching over the balance of the universe."

Bharat closed his eyes against the intense light, feeling the warmth of it wash over him, filling him with a sense of peace and acceptance. When he opened them again, he was standing on Juhu Beach. The cool night air washed over him, and the sound of the waves filled his ears, a soothing, familiar sound that grounded him in the present.

In front of him, the giant ship stood silently, just as it had when he first set foot on it. The sight of it was both comforting and surreal, a reminder of the journey he had just undertaken, of the world he had left behind. The ship seemed almost ordinary now, its grandeur diminished in the soft moonlight, but Bharat knew better. He knew the power it held, the secrets it guarded.

Bharat looked around, unsure if what had just happened was real or a dream. The sand beneath his feet felt solid, the air tasted of salt and sea, and yet there was an otherworldly quality to everything, as if the boundary between the realms had not fully closed. But deep down, he felt a sense of peace, a certainty that Aryavrata was safe and that his journey was far from over.

However, a pang of sadness struck him—he had not gotten a chance to say goodbye to Riya and Aarav, and he missed them deeply. Their faces, their voices, the bond they had formed during their quest—it all felt so vivid, so real, and yet so far away. The thought of never seeing them again, of never sharing another moment of camaraderie and trust, was almost too much to bear.

He wondered what they were doing now, whether they were looking for him, whether they had felt his departure. Did they know that he had been sent back to Earth? Did they understand the sacrifice that had been made? He hoped they did, but the uncertainty gnawed at him, a lingering ache that refused to fade.

Bharat took a deep breath, trying to steady his emotions. He knew that he couldn't dwell on what he had lost—he had a new purpose now, a new role to play in the grand tapestry of the universe. He was a guardian, a Saviour of Realms, and that meant he had responsibilities, duties that transcended his own desires.

As he stood there, watching the waves crash against the shore, Bharat felt a deep resolve settle within him. He would find a way to return to Aryavrata, to see Riya and Aarav again, to fulfill his duty as a guardian. And until that time came, he would protect Earth, his home, with the same determination and courage that had carried him through the trials of Aryavrata.

With one last look at the ship, Bharat turned and began walking along the beach, the sand cool beneath his feet, the wind gentle against his face. The journey wasn't over—far from it. There were still challenges to face, mysteries to unravel, and a world to protect.

But now, as the stars twinkled above him and the ocean whispered its secrets, Bharat felt ready for whatever lay ahead. He was not just a journalist, not just a man caught in extraordinary circumstances. He was a guardian, a Saviour of Realms, and he would embrace that role with everything he had.

And so, with the moonlight guiding his steps and the memories of Aryavrata burning brightly in his heart, Bharat walked on, knowing that his story was far from over.

The Whisper Of Shadows

Life in Mumbai returned to its familiar rhythm, but for Bharat, everything had changed. The bustling city streets, the constant hum of traffic, the vibrant energy of the crowds—it all seemed the same on the surface. Yet, beneath this veneer of normalcy, Bharat felt an undercurrent of something far more profound. The mysterious ship that had captured the attention of the city had vanished from Juhu Beach as suddenly as it had appeared, leaving behind only memories and unanswered questions for those who had witnessed its brief presence.

For the people of Mumbai, the ship became just another oddity, a curious story to tell over dinner or in passing conversations. But for Bharat, the experience had marked the beginning of a journey that had transformed him in ways he could never have imagined. He had returned to his work as a journalist, covering the events and stories of the city as he always had, but his life had taken on a new, hidden dimension. He was no longer just Bharat Verma, the curious and ambitious journalist—he was the guardian of Aryavrata, a protector of the balance between realms.

Though he had returned to his old life, Bharat struggled with the weight of his experiences. His parents had welcomed him home with open arms, but they had noticed the change in him. The first night back, his mother prepared his favourite dinner, dal makhani and fresh rotis, hoping it would bring some warmth back into her son's eyes.

"Bharat, beta," his mother said gently as she placed a plate in front of him, "you've been so quiet since you returned. Is everything alright? What happened to you? Where were you all these days?"

Bharat forced a smile, the smell of the food pulling him back to the comforts of home. "I'm fine, Maa," he replied, his voice steady, though his heart felt heavy. "Just trying to adjust, that's all." He ignored the other questions asked by his mother.

His father, sitting across the table, lowered his newspaper and studied him for a moment. "You've been through something, haven't you?" his father asked, his deep voice resonating with concern. "You can tell us, son. We're here for you."

Bharat hesitated, glancing between his parents, knowing they could never understand the magnitude of what he had endured. How could he explain the battles, the sacrifices, the strange, magical realm of Aryavrata? He had faced Raktashak, nearly given up his own life, and now, his heart still beat with the pulse of that distant realm.

"I missed you both," Bharat said softly, his voice cracking slightly. "I just need time to figure things out."

His mother reached across the table and held his hand, her touch warm and comforting. "Take all the time you need, Bharat," she whispered, "but don't shut us out."

As the dinner continued, Bharat felt a pang of guilt. He loved his parents, but the weight of his new reality made him feel distant, almost disconnected from the life he once knew. How could he go back to being just their son when he was also something more now? The guardian of a realm.

The next day, Bharat met Meera for coffee, their usual spot by Marine Drive. It was a place they had spent countless afternoons, watching the waves crash against the rocks while laughing about work, life, and the future. But today, the air between them was different—heavier.

"You've changed, Bharat," Meera said quietly, stirring her coffee absentmindedly as she studied him across the table. "Ever since that ship... you haven't been the same."

Bharat looked at her, guilt rising in his chest. He couldn't hide it from her, not Meera. They had been through too much together. He wanted to tell her everything, to explain the world he had seen, the sacrifices he had almost made. But how could he drag her into this?

"I've been through something... difficult," Bharat admitted, his voice low. "It's hard to talk about."

Meera's eyes softened with concern, her hand reaching out to touch his across the table. "You don't have to carry it alone, Bharat. Whatever it is, I'm here."

He wanted to tell her that it was impossible—that his new role, his connection to Aryavrata, was something she couldn't understand. But seeing the worry in her eyes, he nodded instead. "I know, Meera. I just need time."

They sat in silence for a while, watching the waves in the distance. Bharat's thoughts drifted back to Aryavrata, to Riya and Aarav. He missed them, missed the sense of purpose that had driven him during their quest. Sitting here with Meera, in a world that was familiar but somehow distant, he felt torn between two lives—one filled with the mundane, and the other with magic, danger, and responsibility.

Though he could not physically return to Aryavrata, Bharat felt its presence within him, a constant connection that pulsed through his very being. It was as if the realm itself had left an indelible mark on his soul, guiding his actions and decisions in subtle ways. He found himself more attuned to the world around him, more sensitive to the shifts and currents of reality that others could not perceive. Yet, despite this newfound awareness, the thought of never seeing Riya and Aarav again weighed heavily on him. He missed the camaraderie they had shared, the bond forged in the crucible of their journey together.

Driven by this connection, Bharat began a new quest, one rooted not in the physical realm but in the pursuit of knowledge. He spent countless hours in libraries, poring over ancient texts, obscure manuscripts, and historical records. He scoured the internet for any mention of other realms or guardians like himself, piecing together fragments of information that might hint at the existence of the hidden worlds he had been told about. He became a regular at the city's archives, digging through dusty tomes and forgotten scrolls, searching for clues that might lead him back to Aryavrata.

His colleagues noticed the change in him—his intense focus, the way his eyes seemed to look beyond the here and now, as if he were searching for something just out of reach. They remarked on how he seemed both more distant and yet more present than ever, as if he were carrying the weight of some great secret. Bharat's reporting became more nuanced, more insightful, as if he were seeing the world through a new lens, one that revealed the hidden layers of reality that most people never noticed.

But despite his best efforts, the answers he sought remained elusive. The more he learned, the more questions arose, and the more he realised how little he truly knew about the vast and mysterious multiverse that lay beyond the boundaries of his own world. It was as if the knowledge he sought was always just beyond his grasp, tantalisingly close yet maddeningly out of reach.

Then, one day, something unexpected happened. As Bharat was walking through the crowded streets of

Mumbai, his mind preoccupied with the latest article he was working on, he passed by a narrow, dimly lit alley that he had never noticed before. Something about the alley caught his attention—perhaps it was the way the light seemed to bend at the entrance, or the faint, almost imperceptible hum that emanated from within.

Drawn by a sense of curiosity and an inexplicable pull, Bharat turned down the alley. The noise of the city faded behind him as he walked deeper into the narrow passage, the air growing cooler and the shadows lengthening around him. At the end of the alley, he found a small, unassuming shop with a wooden sign hanging above the door. The sign, worn with age, bore no name, only a symbol—a spiral that seemed to twist and turn in on itself, pulling the eye inward.

Bharat hesitated for a moment before pushing open the creaking door. The shop was dimly lit, filled with the scent of old wood and incense. Shelves lined the walls, crammed with an eclectic assortment of artifacts, trinkets, and curiosities from all over the world. Some items looked ancient, others modern, but all seemed to hum with a faint, otherworldly energy.

As Bharat's eyes roamed over the shelves, they landed on a small, familiar-looking statue displayed prominently in the window. It was an effigy of Raktashak, the malevolent sorcerer he had faced in Aryavrata. The sight of it sent a jolt of shock through him—how could this artifact from another realm have found its way here, to this obscure shop in Mumbai?

Curious and slightly alarmed, Bharat approached the statue, his mind racing with questions. He reached out to touch it, half-expecting it to vanish like a mirage. But the statue was solid, its surface cool to the touch, the intricate details of Raktashak's twisted form captured in the dark stone.

As he examined the statue, the shopkeeper, an elderly man with a knowing smile, appeared from behind the counter. His eyes twinkled with an intelligence that seemed to see far more than what lay on the surface.

"Are you interested in the statue of Raktashak?" the shopkeeper asked, his voice raspy but kind, as if he already knew the answer.

Bharat's heart skipped a beat. The words were simple, but they carried a weight that suggested the shopkeeper knew more than he was letting on. "Do you know anything about Raktashak?" Bharat asked, his voice barely above a whisper, as if speaking too loudly might shatter the delicate balance of reality.

The shopkeeper simply smiled, a cryptic expression that held both secrets and revelations. Without another word, he turned and returned to attend to other customers, leaving Bharat with more questions than answers.

Feeling a mix of unease and intrigue, Bharat purchased the statue and left the shop, the small effigy wrapped carefully in a cloth. As he stepped back into the bright light of the Mumbai streets, the sounds of the city rushed back to greet him, but the weight of the statue in his hands reminded him that his journey was far from over.

As he walked home, his mind swirled with thoughts. The presence of Raktashak's statue in the shop was no mere coincidence—it was a sign, a warning that the sorcerer's shadow might still loom over Aryavrata and perhaps even other realms. The uneasy feeling in his gut told him that this was just the beginning, that the battles he had fought were only a prelude to the challenges that lay ahead.

Bharat knew that he couldn't ignore this development. The connection between Earth and Aryavrata was still active and the implications were both thrilling and terrifying. His role as a guardian was far from complete, and the delicate balance between worlds was still in danger.

The winds of Juhu Beach continued to whisper their secrets, and as Bharat held the statue close, he knew that as long as those winds blew, his role as a guardian—and his journey—would continue. The story was far from over. New challenges and mysteries awaited him, and he would face them with the same determination and courage that had carried him through the trials of Aryavrata.

And so, with a sense of anticipation and a heart steeled for whatever lay ahead, Bharat walked into the twilight, knowing that the shadows of the past still lingered, and that he was ready to confront them once more.

www.ingramcontent.com/pod-product-compliance
Lightning Source LLC
La Vergne TN
LVHW041103150826
845673LV00007B/1903

* 9 7 9 8 8 9 5 5 6 5 4 1 4 *